THE GUNSMITH

462

The Gypsy King

Books by J.R. Roberts
(Robert J. Randisi)

The Gunsmith series

Lady Gunsmith series

Angel Eyes series

Tracker series

Mountain Jack Pike series

COMING SOON!

The Gunsmith
463 – The Gunsmith's Women's Club

For more information visit:
www.SpeakingVolumes.us

THE GUNSMITH

462

The Gypsy King

J.R. Roberts

SPEAKING VOLUMES, LLC
NAPLES, FLORIDA
2020

The Gypsy King

ISBN 978-1-64540-291-6

Chapter One

Just outside Silverton, Nevada

The posse rode into the gypsy camp, a sheriff and four temporary deputies. A young man stood in front of them.

"What do you want?" he asked.

"I need to speak to your leader," the sheriff said. "Who is that?"

"The King."

"King?" The sheriff looked at his men, who all laughed. "All right, then. Let me talk to your King."

Women and children gathered around the strangers to stare.

The young man said, "Wait here. I will find King Milosh."

"Milosh," the sheriff repeated, under his breath. "What the hell kinda name is that?"

"Hungarian," the young man said, then turned and walked away.

"What the hell is a Hungarian?" the sheriff asked his men.

***

The young man, whose name was Ferka, found King Milosh sitting by a fire, drinking gypsy tea.

"The law is here," he said. "They want to see you."

"Then we better go and see what they want."

Milosh stood and stretched to his full six-foot-two. His shoulder length hair was grey, but prematurely so, as he was just forty. The set of his jaw and lines in his face made him seem older.

He and Ferka walked back to where the mounted posse waited. They were now surrounded not only by women and children, but other men from the camp. The men were armed, but only with knives, no guns.

"Sheriff," Milosh said, "welcome to our camp. Would you and your men like to dismount and have some tea with us?"

"Fuck your tea," the sheriff said. "We're here on business. So, you're the King?"

"I am Milosh. If we were in Hungary, you would call me King Milosh."

"But we ain't in Hungry, wherever that is."

"No, we are not."

"I'm the sheriff of Silverton, and we been havin' some stealin' goin' on."

"And you assume, because we are gypsies, that we are guilty?" Milosh asked.

"Pretty much, yeah," the sheriff said.

"Then you may search our wagons for these stolen items," Milosh said.

The sheriff looked around the camp, at the various fires that were burning.

"Judging by those fires, I'm figurin' you've already eaten some of what you stole."

"Ah, you speak, of animals—pigs? Goats? They wander into our camp of their own volition, and we cook them. I'm sure we have some left, if you would like to partake."

"I don't think so," the sheriff said. "I think you people just better pack up and move on."

"We have only been here a few days—" Milosh started.

"You either pack up and move on," one of the other men said, "or we'll come back and burn ya out."

Milosh seemed puzzled by those words. But rather than address the man who spoke them, he looked at the sheriff.

"Is this how you would choose to enforce your laws?" he asked.

"Look, King whatever your name is," the sheriff said. "It seems to me you and your people have eaten most of the evidence. So I ain't gonna be able to arrest you and prove you stole those chickens and pigs. If some of the farmers and ranchers wanna come out here and burn you out, there ain't gonna be much I can do about it, is there? So my advice to you is to hitch up your wagons and git."

Milosh stared at the sheriff for a few moments, then said, "Before we go, would you or your men like your fortunes told?"

"You've got til mornin'," the sheriff said. "If you ain't gone by then, it's gonna be outta my hands."

The sheriff and his men turned their horses and rode out of the gypsy camp.

***

"Whataya think, Sheriff?" one of the men asked, as they got a distance from the camp.

"I dunno," the sheriff said. "Seems to me that King fella might be a little crazy."

"So what do we do?" one of the other men asked.

"I think you boys better get your torches ready," the sheriff said.

***

As the sheriff and his posse rode away, several men came and stood around King Milosh.

"Do you think they will come to burn us out, Milosh?" one man asked.

"I do not think we should give them the opportunity," King Milosh said, putting his arm around the shoulders of his young son, standing next to him. "I think we should show them what it means to threaten a gypsy."

Chapter Two

Clint Adams was thinking about his new horse.

The animal was a three-year-old Tobiano/Red Roan mix who he had recently purchased, thinking that Eclipse might deserve to be put out to pasture soon after their years together. This had occurred once before, when he was forced to put his big black gelding Duke into retirement. Receiving Eclipse as a gift from P.T. Barnum in New York had been a surprise—even moreso when the Darley Arabian turned out to be Duke's equal.

But what were the chances of finding another horse that could measure up to those two? Not very good, but the Tobiano—tentatively named "Toby," which Clint wasn't thrilled with—was still young, and there was no telling how he would develop as he got older.

For the time being, he had put the horse into the care of his friend John Locke, who had a ranch near Las Vegas, New Mexico. Locke—a man whose ability with a gun had caused him to become known as "The Widowmaker"—was happy to take the horse into his care. Even if he was called away from his ranch, as he often was, he had a foreman who knew his stuff and would take good care of Toby . . .

***

The Widowmaker's foreman was Ben Morton. Clint always found it odd that John Locke called Morton his foreman, since he was also the only hand on the ranch. Not that it really mattered, since there were never more than five or six horses in the corral anytime Clint was there. But they were usually first-rate stock, as Locke knew his horses.

"This one is special," Morton said. He and Clint studied the Tobiano, who was in the corral alone at the moment. The other horses were in the barn.

"I know," Clint said, "that's why I had to have him."

"Who broke him?" Morton asked.

"I did," Clint said, "with Eclipse's help."

"I didn't know you rode broncs."

"I don't," Clint said.

Morton turned his attention from the horse to Clint. He was a tall, slender man in his thirties, who Clint had only met the year before, on his last visit to John Locke's Bar W ranch.

"Then how did you do it?"

"Eclipse and I," Clint said, "we . . . talked to him."

"Talked?"

"Yes."

"And that worked?"

"Eclipse can have that effect on other horses."

"So, if and when you put Eclipse out to pasture," Morton said, "would you be sendin' him here?"

"I don't know," Clint said. "I guess I could discuss that with Locke, the next time I see him."

"He told me you were here last month to drop off the horse," Morton said, "and that you'd be back to check on him. He got called away a couple of days ago, you just missed him."

"Then we can talk about it next time," Clint said. "How are you getting on with Toby?"

"Toby?"

"It's temporary."

"Well," Morton said, "we're gettin' along all right. Locke instructed me not to try to ride him."

"Right," Clint said, "that's for me to do."

"So I've been walkin' him, from time to time," Morton said.

"Any trouble between him and the other horses?" Clint asked.

"Well . . . they don't seem to like him. They cluster together, but he's never among them."

"That's not a problem," Clint said. "Let's put Eclipse in the corral with him and leave them alone for a while."

"We can go inside and have something to eat," Morton said.

Clint had ridden up to the ranch less than an hour before, found Morton standing at the corral, staring at the Tobiano.

"That sounds good."

Clint walked over to where he had left Eclipse standing, removed the saddle and bridle while Morton opened the corral gate. Once he was completely unencumbered, Eclipse trotted over and entered the corral.

Morton closed the gate as Eclipse walked over to where Toby was standing. The two horses hadn't seen each other since Eclipse and Clint had "broken" him. Now they put their heads together and got reacquainted.

Clint walked over and stood next to Morton, again. They watched for a brief time, and then Morton said, "I've got some cold chicken and whiskey in the house."

"Sounds good," Clint said.

They started to walk away, but Morton stopped and turned to look into the corral again.

"Are they gonna be all right?" he asked.

"They'll be fine," Clint said. "We just need to give them some time alone."

"All right," Morton said. "Whiskey and chicken, then."

"Lead the way," Clint said.

Chapter Three

The house was sparsely furnished, as John Locke didn't spend that much time there, and when he did, he was more concerned with his horses.

Morton shared his cold chicken and whiskey with Clint while they caught up on what they had each been doing of late. Morton had simply been working horses, getting them ready for sale, while Clint had been traveling. Since deciding that Labyrinth, Texas would no longer be his fallback home when he was off the trail, Clint needed to find a new place to rest. The town had simply grown too much. His friend Rick Hartman felt the same. So they were both looking for new towns.

"You have a new horse, and you're lookin' for a new town," Morton said. "What about Las Vegas?"

"It's a possibility," Clint said. He had ridden through the town to get to Locke's ranch. It hadn't grown very much since his last few visits.

"You can sleep here in the house tonight," Morton said, while he cleaned up.

"Am I putting you out?" Clint asked.

"Naw, I've got my own room."

"I'm not sleeping in Locke's bed, am I?"

"No, the guest room is yours," Morton said. "Have you never stayed here before?

"The other times, I stayed in a hotel in town."

"Well, I assumed you'd want to be near the Tobiano, so the guest room is set up for you."

"Sounds good."

"But you're gonna have to put up with my cookin' for supper and breakfast."

"I'll make the best of it," Clint said.

"Why don't we go out and see how the horses are doin'?" Morton suggested.

"Suits me," Clint said.

They left the house and walked to the corral, where the Tobiano and Darley Arabian still had their heads together, seemingly standing in the same spot.

"When do you figure to put Eclipse out to pasture and start riding the Tobiano?" Morton asked.

"He's only three." Clint said. "I'd probably wait till he's four or five. Eclipse might be ready for a rest, by then."

"I don't know," Morton said, "that Darley Arabian looks to me like he's got plenty of life left in him."

"Oh, I agree," Clint said, "but when I saw that Tobiano, I just couldn't resist."

"I don't blame you," Morton said. "They're two good-lookin' horses."

"That they are," Clint agreed.

"What else have you got in the barn?" Clint asked.

"Not much, really," Morton said. "A couple of two-year-old colts, and a filly. Not gonna be doin' anythin' with them for a while, so your Tobiano's gonna be gettin' a lot of my attention."

"That's good to hear."

"Where are you headed after you leave here?" Morton asked.

"Don't have anything in mind," Clint said. North, I reckon. Colorado, then maybe either Nevada or Montana."

"Heard somethin' about some rogue gypsies in Nevada burnin' down a town."

"What?"

"That's what I heard when I was in town yesterday," Morton said. "A town called . . . Silverton?"

"I've been to Silverton," Clint said. "Nice little town. Are you sure? I mean, gypsies get blamed for a lot of things."

"I'm just tellin' you what I heard," Morton said.

"Silverton," Clint said, shaking his head. "The sheriff there was a bit of a hard nose, but it was a nice little place. Not far from Virginia City."

"Let's hope the gypsies don't go for Virginia City next," Morton said. "That's a big town."

"I've heard of gypsies picking pockets and telling fortunes," Clint said, "but never burning down a town."

"Like I said," Morton repeated, "it was just somethin' I heard."

"Well," Clint said, "as I go north, I'll be on the lookout for gypsies."

"When will you be leavin'?" Morton asked.

"Tomorrow."

"Then instead of makin' you eat my cookin'," Morton said, "why don't we go into town for supper?"

"And leave this place untended?"

"I got Locke's okay to hire another man," Morton said, "when I need him. I think tonight I'm gonna need 'im."

***

The other man was a broken down lookin' cowpoke named Edmund Fillery. Morton called him Eddie. He was short, bow-legged, and missing pieces of three fingers, which had been bitten off by horses . . .

"Well," he told Clint, holding up his hand, "two by horses, one by an ornery mule."

"So I guess you've been around a lot of animals, then," Clint said.

"My whole life," Eddie said. "Your horses will be fine with me."

Clint wasn't sure about that until Eddie walked to the edge of the corral, and Eclipse came right over to him and nuzzled his injured hand.

He looked at Morton and said, "Let's go to town."

Chapter Four

Clint and Morton rode into Las Vegas, Clint on a borrowed horse. He decided to leave Eclipse with the Tobiano and old Eddie. The three of them would probably get along great.

"How about a beer first?" Morton asked, as they rode down Las Vegas' main street.

"Sounds good."

They stopped in front of The Cactus Saloon.

"It's a simple place," Morton said, as they dismounted. "No gambling, no girls, just beer and whiskey."

"That's all we need right now," Clint said.

They tied off their horses, went inside and approached the bar. There were only a few other men present as the bartender looked at them.

"Two beers," Morton said.

"Sure thing."

"Not much business," Clint said, as the bartender set the beers down in front of them.

"That's what happens when you have no gambling and no girls," the man said.

Clint studied the man. He was in his forties, grim-faced, shoulders slumped as if the weight of the world was on them.

"Isn't that your choice?" he asked.

"Not me," the bartender said. "I just work here. It's the owner who wants to keep this place . . . simple."

"Why work here, then, if you don't like it?" Clint asked.

"Who said I don't like it?" the bartender asked. "It's quiet. Nothin' wrong with that. The place just doesn't make a lot of money. That's the owner's problem."

"What's your name?" Clint asked.

"Oh, sorry," Morton said. "Clint, this is Mike. Mike, this is Clint Adams, a friend of Locke's."

"Ah," Mike said, "the Gunsmith and the Widowmaker are friends. Why doesn't that surprise me?"

"What's your boss's name?" Clint asked.

"Oh, that's Quentin Storm."

"Does he own any other places in town?"

"Another saloon, across town," Mike said. "It's called The Tin Can Saloon."

"Gambling? Girls?" Clint asked.

"All of it," Mike said.

"Have you been there?" Clint asked Morton.

"I have."

"Then why come here?"

"Because all I wanted today was a beer," Morton said. "Then we can go and eat."

"All right," Clint said, "as long as it's a steak."

"Steak it is," Morton said, raising his glass.

***

Morton took Clint to The Branding Iron Steakhouse.

"Best steak in town," Morton promised him, as they entered.

They were shown to a table in the darkened interior of the place, away from windows, and Morton ordered steak dinners for both of them.

"Right away, Mr. Morton," the waiter said.

"You eat here a lot?" Clint asked.

"Locke eats here when he's around," Morton said. "Sometimes I'm with him."

The waiter returned with two frothy mugs of beer. Clint sipped. It was better than what he'd had in the saloon.

"Don't tell me, let me guess," he said. "Quentin Storm owns this place, too?"

"What? No," Morton said. "I do."

"What?"

"That surprise you?"

"Locke pays you enough to open a place like this?" Clint asked.

"Hell, no," Morton said. "I made my fortune long before I met John Locke.

"Then why work for him?"

"We get along," Morton said.

"Does he know about . . . your fortune?"

"He knows I own this place," Morton said, "and that I don't really live off what he pays me. But I like him, and I like working with him and the horses. And look, I met you, and your horses. When would I ever have gotten a chance to work with an animal like Eclipse, or even that Tobiano?" He sipped his beer. "You are gonna change the name, aren't you?"

"Eventually, yes," Clint said.

"Good."

The waiter came with the steak platters and set them down.

"Does he know you own this place?" Clint asked.

"No," Morton said, "nobody who works here does, except my manager."

"And where is he?"

"He stays in the office," Morton said. "Eat up. My cook is the best I could find."

Clint cut into the steak. Juices oozed out, as it was perfectly cooked. He put a piece in his mouth while Morton watched.

"So?"

"It's great," Clint said. "My compliments to your cook."

Chapter Five

Clint found out more about Ben Morton over supper than any other time. He knew enough now to believe that the relationship between Locke and Morton was odd. It seemed as if Locke should be working for Morton, and not the other way around.

"I know what you're thinkin'," Morton said, at one point.

"What's that?"

"What am I doin' workin' for Locke?" Morton said. "He's a good horseman. Me, I'm a businessman who likes horses, so I figured I could learn from him."

"And how is he with business?" Clint asked.

"Lousy," Morton said. "His ranch makes next to nothin', but I know he doesn't care about that. It's just a place for him to hang his hat. Seems to me you're lookin' for a place like that, too."

"I am," Clint said, "but not a ranch. There's too much goes into running a spread. I just need a hotel, some restaurants, and a saloon."

"A nice, quiet town," Morton said.

"Right."

They finished their meal and left the steakhouse.

"So how long do you intend to keep working for Locke?" Clint asked, as they walked. "Doesn't that keep you from your other business?"

"I have people managing my holdings," Morton said. "I trust them. I enjoy working at Locke's ranch. So I guess I'll keep doin' it as long as that continues."

"Makes sense, I guess."

"Don't you have holdings that are being cared for by others?" Morton asked.

"I have a few," Clint said, "but I doubt any of them would interest you."

"We might as well get back to the ranch, see how Eclipse and Toby are doin' with Eddie."

"Let's go."

***

As they rode up to the ranch, Eddie came out of the barn and waited for them.

"How's everythin'?" Morton asked.

"Fine," Eddie said. "I put both of them into stalls. There's only one problem."

"What's that?"

"The other horses don't seem to like them."

Clint and Morton dismounted.

"What?" Clint asked.

"When I took them inside, the other horses got . . . skittish."

Clint looked at the two colts and the filly who were in the corral.

"Is that why they're out here?" he asked.

"Yeah."

"They can't stay out in the corral all night," Morton said.

"Well then," Eddie replied, "somebody has to do something."

"Let me try," Clint said.

"What will you do?" Eddie asked.

"I'll walk them in, see what I can do," Clint said.

"Well, good luck," Morton said. "I've got to go in the house and do some paperwork. Just come on in after you're finished."

"I will."

"Eddie can help you as much as he can," Morton said.

"Sure thing," Eddie said. "Just tell me what you want done."

"Put bridles on the horses in the corral," Clint said.

"Right away."

"I'll see you later," Morton said, and walked to the house.

***

Once the bridles were on the two colts and the filly, Clint led them from the corral into the barn. Or he tried. As they started inside, the three horses began to back away, pulling Clint with them.

"Easy," Clint said. "Take it easy. Come on." He tried to coax them into the barn, but they resisted, and he couldn't budge them.

"All right," he said to Eddie, who was standing by, "let's do this a different way." He handed the reins to Eddie. "Wait here."

He went into the barn and walked to Eclipse's stall.

"Come on, big fella," he said. "I need your help."

He walked the Darley over to the door of the barn, and out. The three ponies stood still as the Darley approached them.

"All right," Clint said, "it's not you who's spooking them, it's Toby."

"How do we fix that?" Eddie asked.

"Let's just see if they'll follow Eclipse inside."

Clint turned the Darley and walked him inside. When Eddie moved forward with the three ponies, they followed. They didn't balk again until they were entirely in the barn.

"Let's put them in stalls as far from Toby as we can," Clint said.

"All right," Eddie said, "let me move him first."

The older man walked to the Tobiano's stall, backed him out, then walked to the end of the barn and into another stall.

Then he came back and took the reins from Clint. He walked the three to the opposite end of the barn from the Tobiano.

"I don't know what it is about him they don't like," Eddie said, as he walked the three horses into their stalls.

"Maybe they're afraid of him?" Clint suggested.

"I understand that even less," Eddie said.

Clint looked at Eclipse, who was standing calmly by.

"So do we put him in a stall next to Toby, or here next to these three?" he wondered aloud.

"Let's try walking him away and see how they react."

Clint nodded. As he started to walk Eclipse toward the Tobiano, the three young horses began to get agitated. They whinnied loudly and shifted their hooves.

Clint turned and brought Eclipse back, and they calmed down.

"Well, that's that," Clint said. He walked Eclipse into a stall right next to the three, leaving Toby at the other end of the barn, alone.

"It doesn't seem to bother them, any," Eddie said. "I guess we're done. If you need me, I'll be in the bunk-house."

Clint nodded, and Eddie left the barn.

Clint walked over to the Tobiano and entered his stall. He stroked the horse's neck.

"I guess you're going to be a loner."

Chapter Six

"Did you fix the problem?" Morton asked as he entered the house

"Yes, and no," Clint said, and then explained.

"But they're all in the barn?" Morton asked.

"Yes, in their own stalls."

"That'll do for now, then."

Morton was sitting at a desk near the front of a window that looked out the front of the house. As Clint stood by the desk, looking out at the corral and barn.

"Where's Eddie?" Morton asked.

"In the bunkhouse."

Morton nodded, studying the papers in front of him.

"I still have some work to do, here," he said. "But we can have a whiskey on the porch later, before we turn in. Just give me a couple of hours."

"Fine," Clint said. "I'll be in the guest room until then."

Morton nodded, and Clint went upstairs to the second floor of the house.

There were three bedrooms up there. Locke's, Morton's and a guest room. He didn't know the size of the other two, but the guest room was spacious. It even had a writing desk by the window.

His saddlebags were on the bed, where they'd been put for him. He sat next to them and fished out the book he was currently reading, Edgar Allan Poe's *The Narrative of Arthur Gordon Pym of Nantucket.*

***

When Clint came back downstairs, Morton was standing behind the desk, stretching.

"I'm not cut out for paperwork," he admitted. "I'd rather ride a horse, bareback. Wait."

He walked to a sideboard and poured two glasses of whiskey, then turned and held them aloft.

"Unless you'd rather have brandy. I think Locke has some of it around here."

"No, the whiskey's fine," Clint said. He wasn't a whiskey drinker, but he preferred it to brandy.

"Then let's go out and sit on the porch."

Morton handed Clint his glass, and they walked outside together and sat in a couple of wicker chairs.

"Who the hell invented this shit?" Morton asked.

"Wicker?" Clint asked. "I think it was the Egyptians."

"I hate it," Morton said, trying to get comfortable. Finally, he stopped, sighed and sipped his whiskey. They looked out at the dark shape of the barn in the night.

"We're gonna have to go out and check on them," Morton said, "before we turn in."

"I can do that, if you like."

"Naw," Morton said, "we'll do it together. The To-biano's gonna have to get to know me for after you and Eclipse are gone."

"I'll need him to get to know me, too," Clint said, "so agreed, we'll go together."

"After we finish these," Morton said, sipping his whiskey again. "You know, I tried to buy this place from Locke."

"When?"

"A while back," Morton said. "Made him one offer."

"He turned you down?"

"He almost killed me," Morton said. "But we got over it, and stayed friends, and I never did that again. He loves this place."

"There'll be a time when he doesn't want to be the Widowmaker anymore," Clint said. "When that time comes, he'll stay here."

"What about a time when you don't want to be the Gunsmith, anymore?"

"I don't have a choice," Clint said.

"Is this about that legend business?"

"I'm afraid so," Clint said.

"You don't like bein' a legend, do you?"

"I don't admit to being one," Clint said.

"From what Locke tells me," Morton said, "and what I read in the newspapers, men like you and Hickok and Bat Masterson don't get much of a choice in the matter."

"I guess not," Clint said.

"Cigar?" Morton asked.

"No thanks."

The man lit one up.

"The part of being on this ranch I like the best is the horses," Morton said, "but this is my second favorite part. Just sittin' here with a drink and a cigar."

"Does Locke ever sit out here with you?" Clint asked.

"Naw," Morton said, "he's got too much energy to relax. I only do this when he's not around."

"Well," Clint said, "I'll keep your secret."

"I appreciate it," Morton said.

Clint stood.

"I'm gettin' an early start so I'll go and check the horses, and then say goodnight. If you want to stay here and relax—"

"No, no," Morton said, "I'll tag along, then come back here when you turn in." He stood up. "I'm always up with the sun, so you'll get breakfast before you go."

"Sounds good."

They headed for the barn.

Chapter Seven

Eight days later, Clint bypassed Denver because he knew his friend, Talbot Roper, was away on a case. The best private detective in the country was often called away, so Clint decided to just keep moving.

When he crossed the border from Colorado into Wyoming, he headed west, as he had been to Laramie recently and didn't relish returning there any time soon.

He camped just south of Sweetwater and Rock Springs, then after a breakfast of coffee and bacon the next morning, decided to bypass both those towns. He knew neither of them would suit his needs.

He had been riding west for about an hour when he heard the sound of horses pounding somewhere ahead of him. It sounded like six or eight of them, maybe a posse. There were no shots, though. Usually a pursuing posse is throwing shots at somebody. This bunch might have just been trying to close the gap between themselves and whoever they were chasing.

When he finally came within sight of them, he saw that he was right. He counted six riders but was surprised to see they were chasing a single figure who was on foot. When he saw a flash of skirt and bright colors, he knew it was a woman. Posse or not, he didn't like what he was seeing, so he urged Eclipse on, hoping to get between the riders and the running woman.

He had to move fast, as the riders were quickly catching up to the woman, who appeared to be running pretty fast. She had her skirt pulled up enough that he could see a flash of legs, and he realized it was more of a girl than a woman.

She had long, dark hair, and appeared to be wearing a blouse that revealed her shoulders. Clint wondered if this was, indeed, a posse, or just a bunch of men with something nasty in mind.

Because Eclipse was so fast, he was able to get between the girl and the riders, just as she lost her balance and tumbled to the ground. If Clint hadn't been there, the riders might have trampled her, but seeing him, the six of them pulled up and stopped short. As the dust settled, Clint and the riders regarded each other. Clint didn't see any badges.

"You're in the way, Mister!" one man shouted at him.

Clint ignored the man, turned and looked at the girl, who was getting to her feet.

"Are you all right?" he asked her.

"Yes," she snapped, "I am fine." She began dusting herself off from her fall.

"Mister, I'm talkin' to ya!" the man shouted.

Clint turned and looked at the spokesman, riding Eclipse to get closer to the group.

"I was just checking to see if the lady was all right," he said.

"Lady?" The man and his colleagues all started to laugh. Most of them looked to be in their thirties, a couple might've been in their twenties. "She ain't no lady. She's a goddamned gypsy."

Clint turned to look over his shoulder. The girl was standing with her hands on her hips, glaring at the six men. Her long, dark hair was in disarray and he could see the large hoop earrings she was wearing. From the little experience Clint had with gypsies, she certainly looked the part.

"What I see is a young lady on foot being chased by six men on horseback. Doesn't seem very fair to me."

"Fair's got nothin' to do with it," the spokesman said. "She's a little thief."

"I don't see any badges on your chests," Clint said, "so you're not a posse."

"We don't need no badges," the man said. "She stole from two of us, and we aim to take it out of her hide."

"I hope that doesn't mean what it sounds like," Clint said.

"Mister, you better stand aside," the man said. "We aim to have her."

"Now, that definitely does sound like you intend to rape her."

The man grinned.

"Let's just say we intend to take it out in trade."

"I don't think so," Clint said.

"Mister," the man said, "there's six of us and only one of you."

"I tell you what," Clint said. "I'll just wait here while you go and get some more help."

Chapter Eight

The six men looked at Clint like he had lost his mind.

"Mister," the head man said, "you're tryin' our patience."

"If you think she's a thief," Clint asked, "why don't you have a lawman with you?"

"Because she's a damn gypsy!" the man snapped. "She don't deserve no white man's law."

"Well," Clint said, "we're not in agreement there. I tell you what, I'll just take her back to her people, and you can have a lawman go out there to talk to them. You got a lawman where you're from, don't you?"

"Yeah, we got a lawman in Rock Springs," the man said. "But he ain't involved."

"Well, you just better get him involved," Clint said. "None of you are putting a hand on this girl."

"It ain't our hands we wuz thinkin' about puttin' on her," one of the other men said. He looked to be the youngest in the group.

"You might think you're funny, son," Clint said, "but I don't."

"Now Mister," the leader said, "this's gone far enough. Get the hell out of the way."

"I can't do that," Clint said.

"You ready to die for a gypsy girl?"

"I'll kill the first man who touches his gun," Clint said, "and then you'll be next."

"You got a lot of confidence in yerself, Mister," the leader said.

"I'll take 'im, Lonny," the young one said, riding up next to "Lonny."

"Don't touch your gun, boy," Clint said. "I'm warning you."

"Easy," Lonny said to the kid. "We'll take him together."

"There aren't enough of you," Clint said.

"Goddamn, you're confident!" Lonny snapped. "Who the hell are you, anyway?"

"My name's Clint Adams."

All six mounted men seemed to take a mental step back. They stared at him.

"The Gunsmith?" Lonny asked, shifting in his saddle.

"That's right."

"W-what are you doin' here?" Lonny asked.

"I'm about to kill six stupid cowpokes," Clint said.

"If you really are the Gunsmith," the young one said. "Can you prove it?"

"I can."

"How?"

"By killing six stupid cowpokes."

"Now wait—" Lonny said.

"He can't," the young one said. "Even if he is the Gunsmith, he can't kill all of us."

"Danny, shut up!" Lonny ordered.

"Danny could be right," Clint said. "One of you might get me, but I'd get the other five."

"If you're the Gunsmith," Danny said.

"We're still on that?"

There was a trick Clint had done many times before, even though he didn't like trick shooting. But sometimes it served a purpose.

He drew quickly and fired twice. Lonny and Danny's holster flew off their hips and fell to the ground, with the guns still in them.

Clint quickly replaced the spent shells and holstered his own weapon.

"Holy . . ." Lonny breathed.

"The girl is coming with me," Clint said.

"Oh, yeah, sure," Lonny said.

"Anybody else object?"

None of the other men spoke, and young Danny looked incapable of speaking. He was still shocked.

"Then turn around and ride away," Clint said. "Now!"

Lonny looked down at his gun, lying on the ground.

"Come back for that later," Clint said. "Now go!"

The other four riders immediately turned their horses and started away. Slowly, as if they were incapable of moving any faster, Lonny and Danny followed. Clint sat there watching them until they were far enough away for him to turn.

The girl was standing there, also looking at him with shocked eyes.

"I—I have never seen anything like that before," she said.

"Is it true?" he asked.

"That I am a gypsy?" she asked. "Yes."

"No," Clint said, "is it true that you stole from them?"

"Oh that," she said, with a shrug. "Yes, that is true."

"Why?" he asked.

"I am a gypsy," she said, as if that should explain everything.

"What did you steal?"

"Food," she said, "a purse."

"Money?"

"Very little," she said. "But I did not have any others to choose from. It was those six who approached me."

"What did they want?"

She put her hands on her hips, thrusted out her chest and lifted her chin.

"What do you think, *Gadjo*?"

36

Chapter Nine

Clint reached down and pulled the girl up behind him.

"This is a magnificent animal," she said.

"What's your name?" he asked.

"Ayesha."

"Where are your people, Ayesha?" he asked.

She pointed.

"That way."

Clint started in the direction she was pointing.

"How will your people receive me when we get there?" Clint asked.

"You will be welcomed," Ayesha said. "We are a friendly people. Also, you saved me. The King will be pleased."

"King?"

"King Milosh."

"And just why will he be so pleased?"

She slid her arms around him and held him tight.

"He is my father," she said.

"Ah, the King's daughter," Clint said. "How's he going to feel when he finds out what you've been doing?"

"He'll be very proud," she said. "I will have shown him I am as valuable as a son."

"Does he have any sons?"

"Yes, three," she said. "And he loves them all more than he does me."

"So you went out to try to earn daddy's love?"

"Something like that."

"Do you think it'll work?"

"Probably not," she said. "In fact, if you don't want to take me back to them, it's fine with me." She pressed up against him so that he felt her breasts, and her nipples, against his back. "I'm fine with going away with you."

"That's all right," he said. "I'll take you back."

She fell quiet for the rest of the ride . . .

***

As they approached the gypsy camp, Clint saw about a half dozen wagons, different styles shapes and ages, a rag-tag looking wagon train. There were about twenty-five people milling about, including women and children.

"Is this all of your people?" he asked.

"All of them in this country," she said.

As they approached, people noticed them, stopped what they were doing and gave the two all their attention. Their expressions were curious, as they hadn't yet seen it was Ayesha riding behind Clint.

"Will they open fire on me?" Clint asked.

"No," Ayesha said, "we are a peaceful people. They'll welcome you," she reminded him.

"That's good."

More people began to gather around, watching the both of them.

"Which one's the King," he asked, looking around, "your father?"

"He's not there," she said, "but he will be."

Clint stopped about ten feet away from the assembled people, reached back and lowered Ayesha to the ground. When the crowd saw her, they smiled, and one woman stepped forward. She was easily as beautiful as Ayesha, though about twenty years older.

"Ayesha," she said. "We were so worried." The two women embraced.

"I was in a lot of trouble," Ayesha said, "running on foot, but this man saved me. He got between me and six men and ran them off."

The woman looked at Clint.

"We are very appreciative," she said. "Would you step down and eat with us?"

"I don't mind if I do, Ma'am," Clint replied, and dismounted.

"That is an amazing looking animal," the woman said. "Vano can take him for you."

A young man stepped up.

"Be careful," Clint said, handing over Eclipse's reins. "He'll bite you."

"Vano is very good with horses," the woman said. "They will get along."

Clint watched as the young man stroked Eclipse's neck and spoke to the Darley in a low tone. Then the two walked away together, calmly.

"Come with us," the woman said. "The King will want to meet you."

"King Milosh?"

"That's right."

"And who are you?"

"I am Varna."

"Queen Varna?"

The woman smiled.

"Just Varna." She linked her arm into Ayesha's. "Follow us."

Chapter Ten

He followed the two women to the largest wagon in the camp.

Once there, Varna released Ayesha's arm and entered the wagon through its rear door. The rest of the wagons were all covered Conestogas. This was the only one with walls and a door, a former peddler's wagon.

When the door opened again, Varna stepped out, followed by a stocky, powerfully built man wearing a headband and earrings. His colorful shirt had billowing sleeves, his pants were leather and his boots worn. He looked to be in his fifties.

"Father," Ayesha said.

He smiled and opened his arms. She ran into his embrace. Varna stood by, smiling.

"Welcome back, my daughter."

"Milosh, this is the man who rescued her," Varna said.

"From six men, father."

"We are grateful," Milosh said to Clint. "I am Milosh."

"King Milosh, the way I hear it."

"If we were home, yes," the man said. "Here I am simply Milosh. And you are?"

"Clint Adams."

"I know that name," Milosh said. "You are the Gunsmith. That explains how you were able to save my daughter from six men."

"I just did my best," Clint said.

"Well, apparently that was good enough," Milosh said. "Varna tells me she invited you to eat with us. And you accepted."

"That's true."

"Then will you spend the night with us?"

Clint hesitated.

"We can give you a wagon," Milosh said. "You will have privacy."

"Sounds good," Clint said.

"Varna will take you there," Milosh said. "And she will come and get you when it is time to eat. Then we can talk and get better acquainted."

"I'll take him to the wagon," Ayesha offered.

"No," her father said, "we must talk. I must know everything that happened since you left." He looked at the older woman. "Varna."

"Mr. Adams," Varna said.

"Call me Clint."

"Very well," Varna said. "This way, Clint."

* * *

Clint saw that they had assumed he would accept their invitation, since his saddlebags and rifle were already in the wagon.

"Do you need anything?" Varna asked.

"Just to wash up."

"There is a barrel on the side of this wagon," Varna told him.

"Then I'm good."

She smiled.

"I will come and get you when it is time to eat," she said.

"I'll look forward to it."

She stepped away and allowed the back flap of the wagon to drop. As promised, he had privacy.

He found a towel, took it outside with him, washed up in the barrel of water, and dried off. Then he went back inside the wagon to think.

Just because he'd heard a story about some gypsies burning down the town of Silverton, Nevada didn't mean it was these gypsies who did it. Granted, they weren't all that far from Silverton. It was about three hundred and sixty miles, but that could've been covered by the wagons in less than a month. He wasn't sure when Silverton had been burned, but that'd be cutting it close.

He was sitting, wondering what his next move should be, when he heard someone outside his wagon.

"Clint?"

It was Varna. He opened the flap.

"It is time to eat," she said.

***

When he reached the fire, there was a pig on a spit being rotated by a plain looking woman who smiled up at him.

"This is Sasha," Varna said. "She does most of our cooking."

"Hello," Clint said.

"It is almost ready," Sasha said to him. "I will pour you some tea."

He looked at Varna.

"Gypsy tea," she said. "It is probably more . . . potent than you have had in the past."

"Sounds interesting," he said, accepting a cup from Sasha. He sipped it, kept himself from choking. "I see what you mean," he managed to say.

"It is time for me to carve," Sasha said.

Suddenly there was a mob of people around the fire, all holding plates.

Chapter Eleven

The pig was cooked to perfection by Sasha. While there were plates to eat it from, there were no knives or forks, so everyone simply ate with their fingers. It was not a problem for Clint, since they gave him a huge hunk of meat he could easily hold.

"How is it?" Milosh asked.

"It's great," Clint said, then looked at Sasha. "My compliments."

"Thank you."

He looked back at Milosh, who ate voraciously, his mouth and chin covered with grease.

"And the tea?" Varna asked.

"Like you said," Clint replied, "it's got more of a kick to it."

"Wait until you've had a gypsy steak," Milosh said.

"And when would that be?"

"As soon as we steal a cow," Milosh said, laughing. "Oh, I mean, as soon as one wanders into our camp." He held his finger to his lips and laughed again.

All right, so they stole things. That still didn't mean they burned down a town. But maybe they knew who did. Clint put the question aside until later and went back to enjoying the excellent pork. By the time he was done, he was sure his own face was covered with grease as well.

"That was great," Clint said, handing Sasha his plate. "Thank you."

"More tea?" she asked.

"No, thanks," he said. "I'm more of a beer man."

"You will have to go to town for that," Milosh said, "and from what my daughter tells me, we would not be welcomed."

"Tell me something, Milosh," Clint said, "did you actually send your daughter to town to steal?"

"You make it sound worse than it really is," Milosh said. "It was simply a . . . rite of passage."

"So she wasn't stealing for the sake of stealing," Clint observed.

"Mr. Adams—"

"Clint."

"Clint . . . gypsies have long been mislabeled," Milosh said. "We are a peace-loving people who make our way in this world the best we can."

"So stealing is not a way of life for you?"

"Hardly," Milosh said. "and I hope by the time you leave us, you will understand."

Clint hoped the same thing.

***

Alone in his wagon, he lit the lamp they had given him and reclined on his bedroll. So far, the gypsies seemed like decent, inviting people, just as King Milosh described them. As a man with a reputation, he knew how people could describe a person or group in an uncomplimentary light. He had certainly suffered that himself. And everything he'd heard or thought he knew about gypsies indicated the same was true of them.

Since he was in unfamiliar territory, he kept his boots on, remained dressed and kept his gun close at hand. When someone knocked on the side of his wagon, he grabbed his gun and sat up straight.

"Who is it?"

"Ayesha," she said, pulling the flap aside so she could look in. "May I come in?"

"I don't think your father would like that, Ayesha," Clint said. "I'm going to have to say no."

She pouted prettily.

"I thought you might be lonely."

"It's a nice thought," Clint said, "and I thank you."

"But you are turning me away?" she asked.

"Ayesha," he said, "you're very young, and your father is around here, somewhere, and I noticed that he wears not one, but two knives. So yes, I'm turning you away."

She pouted again, then huffed off.

Clint sat back and breathed in the fragrance Ayesha had left in her wake.

He had only just slid his gun back in its holster when someone else knocked on the side of the wagon.

"Yes?"

The flap was pulled aside and King Milosh appeared, smiling. Clint wondered if he had seen his daughter stomping off.

"I thought you might like something a little stronger than tea before you turn in," Milosh said.

"That sounds good."

The King climbed in and brandished a metal flask.

"It is not gypsy, but it *is* whiskey," he said.

Clint accepted the flask and took a stiff swig. The whiskey burned its way down as he returned the flask to Milosh, who then took a healthy swig.

"I also wanted to warn you," the King said.

"About what?"

"Ayesha," Milosh said. "My daughter can be . . . precocious, at times."

"Is that right?"

"Oh, yes," Milosh said. "It would not surprise me if she tries to sneak into your wagon tonight."

"Thanks for the warning," Clint said. "I'll keep my eyes open."

Milosh held up the flask, but Clint shook his head.

"Then I will allow you to turn in," Molish said. "Good night."

He left the wagon, allowed the flap to fall back into place, and Clint was alone again.

Temporarily . . .

***

He was drifting off the next time somebody knocked on the side of the wagon.

"May I come in?" Varna asked, peeling the flap back and smiling at him.

"I guess that depends," he said.

"On what?"

"Are you married to King Milosh?"

"I am not."

"Then come on in."

Chapter Twelve

Varna climbed aboard the wagon, allowed the flap to close behind her. Her aroma filled the interior. It was similar to Ayesha's, but more potent, sensuous. The older woman had what it would take Ayesha years to develop.

"Why did you ask me if I am married to the King?" she asked, settling down across from him.

"I don't want to do anything to offend him," Clint said, "like being alone with his wife, or daughter."

"Ayesha was here?"

"Yes, she offered to . . . keep me company."

"She is impetuous," Varna said. "But she is a smart girl."

"I can see that."

"And she is nineteen."

"I told her she was too young when I sent her away," Clint said. "She wasn't happy."

"But I'm sure King Milosh was."

"Yes," Clint said, "he came by to offer me a drink before turning in."

"He appreciates what you did for his daughter."

"Saving her?"

Varna smiled.

"And turning her away."

"Ah."

"He wants you to have a pleasant night."

"So he sent you?"

She smiled and produced something from the folds of her skirt—a flask.

"With this."

"I see."

She handed it to him, and he took a swig before handing it back. She took a deep drink.

"So what is your place here, if not Queen?" he asked.

"There is no Queen," she said. "Just an exiled King."

"And how does he feel about being exiled?" Clint asked.

"Honestly, he is more . . . self-exiled."

"He did it to himself?"

"Well," she said, "it was either that, or be killed. So, he came here and brought some of his loyal followers with him."

"I suppose it's important for even an exiled King to have loyal subjects," Clint said.

"Yes, it is."

She passed him the flask again and they once again exchanged drinks. Her demeanor became more languid as she stretched out before him.

"Wait," Clint said, "are you telling me the King sent you to me?"

"Sent me," she said, "allowed me. It's all the same. We want you to be comfortable. If I don't suit you, there are others . . . but I volunteered."

"You did?"

"Of course," she said. "You are the Gunsmith, you should have only the best we have to offer."

She lifted her skirt so he could see her smooth, bare legs—then lifted it higher to show that her hair was coal black everywhere. She also began to exude a more pungent aroma, one that he found very familiar.

She released her skirt so she was partially covered again, except for her ankles and calves. Then she began to rub her fingertips along the bodice of her peasant blouse.

"Varna—"

"You don't want me to leave, do you?" she asked.

She reached down with both hands, grasped the hem of the blouse, pulled it over her head and tossed it aside. Her breasts were large, with heavy undersides and very dark nipples.

"Do you?" she asked again, running her fingertip over those nipples.

"Hell, no," he said.

Chapter Thirteen

The wagon they had given Clint for the night was set away from the rest of the camp. He didn't know why, but as he and Varna got out of their clothes and came together in a hot embrace, he was grateful. Hopefully, no one was going to see the wagon bouncing about on its axles.

When Varna was naked, it was clear she was a woman built for sex. She was full-bodied, with the kind of breasts and hips and buttocks Clint wanted to spend a few days in bed with. In addition, she obviously had an appetite that matched her charms.

When they were naked, she threw herself on top of him, using her weight to take him down onto his back. Her flesh was silky smooth and steaming hot. His cock was fully hard and trapped between them as she kissed him, crushing her large breasts against his chest.

The kisses went on for some time, growing hotter and wetter and longer. Then she broke the kiss and pressed her breasts to his face, so he could take the large nipples into his mouth as she moaned and rubbed her hairy pussy up and down his hard shaft. The coarse hair between her legs felt glorious on the tender flesh of his penis, and then suddenly she gushed and wet him with a fluid that felt like hot, smooth honey. She continued to rub up and down on him, and then sat up and took his cock into her steamy depths.

She began to move up and down on him, and that was when he started to feel the wagon bouncing on its axles. Varna didn't seem to be aware of anything but the part of him that was inside of her. She jumped up and down on him, coming down harder and harder, which made her breasts do marvelous things he couldn't stop watching. They jiggled and bounced and . . . rippled. He watched until he couldn't wait anymore, then reached for them. He tried to hold their weight in his hands, but her movements became more and more frantic, making it difficult. Instead he put his hands on her hips and tried to match her, lifting his butt off the bed each time she came down on him, causing her to gasp and moan and bite her lips, so as not to cry out.

Then waves of pleasure took her over, draining her of all her strength until she fell down on him, crushing him beneath her glorious weight and breathing heavily into his ear . . .

***

Outside the wagon, King Milosh watched with pleasure as the wagon bounced about. Varna was doing exactly what he had sent her in there to do, and he knew she was enjoying it, because she was a woman who reveled in sex. And Clint Adams was a man, so he was enjoying himself, as well. Hopefully, by morning, Adams would be totally obsessed with Varna. If the sex didn't accomplish that, Milosh was going to have to try something a bit more old-fashioned.

Like a spell.

For that he would need the old woman, Ethelinda . . .

***

Ethelinda allowed him to enter her wagon. He sat across from her and told her what he wanted.

"This man, this Gadjo," the wizened old woman said, "he is endeared, is he not?"

"He is . . . famed," Milosh said. "A legend, they say."

"And you want me to put a spell on him?" she asked.

"Yes."

"For what purpose?"

"To control him," he said. "I believe we might need his help."

"Why don't you just request his help?" she asked.

"I could do that," Milosh said. "If being with Varna doesn't work—"

"You sent Varna to him?"

"I did, yes."

"Well," she said, "then why do you need me?"

"He is a man who has known many women," Milosh said. "Varna may not be able to . . . possess him."

"There is a man who can resist Varna?" Ethelinda asked.

"Not many," Milosh said. "You know how that feels."

"That was many, many years ago for me," Ethelinda said. "Now it is Varna's turn to carry that . . . curse."

"A curse," Milosh said, with a shrug, "a blessing, some see it differently."

"You know what I will need to cast the spell," she said.

"A lock of his hair."

"Yes."

"I'm sure Varna can supply that."

"If it is needed," Ethelinda said, "I will be ready."

"I will talk to Varna in the morning," he said.

"She will be with this man all night?"

"I'm sure she will."

"If she does not possess him," Ethelinda said, "I will be . . . amazed."

Milosh got to his feet.

"I will let you know," he assured her. "Good-night to you."

Chapter Fourteen

Clint woke and looked over at Varna, whose naked form was lying with her back to him. He reached his hand out to touch her but stopped short. He wasn't finished admiring the graceful line of her back that led to her fulsome buttocks. She made his mouth water.

Finally, though, he had to reach out and run his hand over those firm globes of her butt. She moaned and pressed back against his touch, then rolled over, bringing her big, juicy breasts into view.

"You're a gorgeous woman," he said, moving his hands to her nipples.

"You are a wonderful man," she said. "Then she sat up straight suddenly. "It is morning."

"Yes."

"I must go."

She hastily donned her skirt and peasant top.

"I'm sorry," she said. "We all have our morning duties to perform."

"That's all right," he said, "I'm very pleased with your nighttime duties."

She kissed him, then slid out the back of the wagon to the ground.

***

King Milosh was waiting outside his wagon for Varna.

"Well?" he said.

"I did as you asked," she assured him.

"And?"

"And we will see."

"Did he wake this morning obsessed with you?"

"He woke in a very good mood," she said. "For the rest, we will have to wait."

"Ethelinda is anxious to know," he said.

"No," she said, "you did not go to Ethelinda already."

"I did."

"Milosh, you must give me time."

"We may not have time," he said. "Having the Gunsmith ride into our midst is a fortuitous event. We must take full advantage of it."

"But one night—"

"When have you ever needed more than one night to enchant a man?" Milosh asked.

"This is a special man, Milosh," Varna said. "Do not underestimate him."

"The reason I want his help is because I do *not* underestimate him."

"I must have a bath before I start the day," Varna said.

"You have chores," he reminded her.

"Yes, and one chore is to cast my spell—*my* spell, not Ethelinda's—over Clint Adams, which I cannot do if I am a mess." She put her hands in the mass of tangle her black hair was at the moment.

"Go, then," Milosh said. "I will meet Clint Adams for breakfast and make my own judgment on how well you did last night."

"I do not think you will hear any complaints," Varna said, and walked away.

Milosh also doubted he would hear any complaints, but he wanted more than that. He wanted Clint Adams to be enthralled . . .

***

Clint got dressed, and the first thing he did when he left the wagon was check in on Eclipse to make sure the Darley Arabian had been well cared for.

"He is doing fine," the young man, Vano, told him, while stroking Eclipse's neck.

"I can see that," Clint said. "He doesn't let a lot of men even touch him, let alone stroke him."

"When will you be leaving?" Vano asked.

"Probably after breakfast."

"I will have him ready for you."

"Thank you, Vano."

Clint left the young man and Eclipse and walked into the main part of the camp. He found King Milosh sitting at a fire, drinking from a cup that was probably tea, even though he could smell coffee.

"You have a choice this morning," Milosh told him.

"Do I?" Clint asked, wondering if the comment had anything to do with Varna?

"Yes," Milosh said. "Coffee or tea."

"Oh," Clint said, "I'll take coffee."

"I thought so."

Milosh waved at the woman who was tending the fire, and she handed Clint a cup of coffee.

"Thank you," he said, and she nodded.

He sat down across from King Milosh and then accepted a plate of food from the woman. He noticed there was no one else eating breakfast with the King.

"Is this a gypsy delicacy?" he asked.

"It is," the King said, "it's called bacon-and-eggs."

Clint started eating.

Chapter Fifteen

"I'll be leaving right after breakfast," Clint told Milosh.

"Really?" Milosh asked. "To go where?"

"Probably to Rock Springs."

"That would be good," Milosh said. "We need some help there."

"Have you been to Rock Springs?"

"No," Milosh said, "but as you know, Ayesha has. And now she cannot go back, and she cannot be seen by those men. Unless . . ."

"Unless what?"

"Unless you can convince them that gypsies are not bad people."

"So you want me to represent you in Rock Springs?" Clint asked.

At that point Varna appeared, looking fresh from a bath. Her hair was clean and lustrous.

"Ah," she said, "breakfast."

The old woman handed her a plate of food and a cup of gypsy tea.

"I was just talking with Clint about going to Rock Springs to help us."

"Would you do that?" she asked Clint, with wide eyes. "For us?"

"Wait, wait . . . you admitted to me you sent Ayesha there to steal."

"Well . . ." Milosh said.

Varna leaned forward and put her hand on Clint's arm. When he looked at her, she appeared to be trying to peer into his soul. He had a feeling he knew what last night, and this morning, had all been about.

"We need your help," she said. "Don't you want to help us, Clint?"

He smiled at her, ate the last piece of bacon from his plate.

"I'll have to go to Rock Springs before I make up my mind about that," he said.

Varna removed her hand, sat back and looked at King Milosh.

"Then we will wait," Milosh said.

Clint stood up.

"Thank you for letting me spend the night, for the meals and . . . all," he said.

"We will remain camped here as long as we can," Milosh said.

"If you have to move," Clint said, "it shouldn't be too hard for me to find you."

"I believe that," Milosh said.

Clint looked at Varna, who was now concentrating on her breakfast.

"I'll let you know if I decide to help you or not," he promised, and went to saddle Eclipse.

***

Before he could mount up and leave, Ayesha came running up to him.

"You're leaving?"

"It's time."

"But you and me," she said, "we ain't got to know each other."

"I told you, Ayesha," he said. "You're very young." He looked over at Vano, who seemed to be watching the young girl very closely.

"Seems to me you've got some young men here who'd like to get to know you better."

"I'm not interested in any of them," she said.

"You know," Clint said, "you don't look much like your father."

"I know it."

"You favor your mother?"

"I don't know," she said. "I never knew her."

He studied her, her light skin and auburn hair. Her clothes said gypsy, but that was all. He wondered.

"I'll be back, Ayesha," he said, mounting up.

"You promise?"

"I do."

"Honest?"

"I'm not a gypsy," he said. "I don't steal or lie."

He whipped Eclipse around and rode out of camp.

***

"You don't have him," Milosh said to Varna as Clint rode out.

"I told you," she said. "I just needed a little more time."

"Well, we don't have it," he said. "Did you get what Ethelinda will need?"

She hesitated, then put her hand in the pocket of her skirt and brought out a lock of hair, which she passed over to King Milosh.

"He didn't feel it?"

"When I pulled it out," she said, "he was feeling a lot of things."

Chapter Sixteen

Rock Springs was a good-sized town with enough shops and saloons to satisfy any man. He reined in Eclipse in front of the Touchstone Hotel, went in and got himself a room, then came out to find a livery and board the Darley. Then he walked back to the hotel with his saddlebags and rifle. If the desk clerk had recognized his name in the register, he wasn't showing it. But he was a middle-aged gent who probably knew enough to mind his own business.

It was early and the streets were busy with people coming and going. After leaving his gear in his room, he left his hotel, dodged a couple of buckboards while crossing the street, and entered The Wild Mustang Saloon.

At mid-afternoon, the place was about half full. Clint looked around. The clientele seemed to be a combination of ranch hands and townspeople. The men who had been chasing Ayesha looked like they had come from a ranch, but he didn't see any familiar faces, so he stepped to the bar.

"Beer," he said.

"Comin' up," the barkeep said.

He set a cold beer down in front of Clint.

"You do a pretty good business this early in the day," Clint commented.

"We're popular," the bartender said. "Wait til later when the girls come down."

Clint looked around again, still didn't see any familiar faces.

"You lookin' for somebody?" the bartender asked.

Clint turned his attention back to the man.

"I heard something about gypsies in this area," he said.

The bartender didn't react.

"I hate gypsies," Clint said. "I wouldn't want to be in a saloon that served them."

The bartender grinned.

"You got nothin' to worry about here," he assured Clint. "This whole town hates gypsies. In fact, we almost got to hang one for stealin'."

"Is that right?"

"Yeah," the bartender said. "Thought she'd get away with it because she was a girl. Some of the hands from the Circle K chased her down, and almost had her, but they was run off by a bunch of 'em with guns. You believe that? Gypsies with guns."

Obviously, the Circle K boys didn't want anyone to know that they had been run off by a single man.

"That's too bad," Clint said.

"But the boys are gonna go out again, this time with more men. When they find 'em, they'll take care of 'em."

"What about the law?" Clint asked. "Won't they have anything to say about it?"

"Marshal Fredericks told 'em not to take the law into their own hands," the bartender said, "but they ain't about to listen. Fredericks is gettin' up there in years, and he'll be replaced soon."

Clint finished his beer and put the empty mug down.

"Thanks for the information," he said. "I'll be back later to see the girls."

"Take my word for it," the bartender said, "it's gonna be crowded."

"Oh, I believe you," Clint said, and touched the brim of his hat.

***

He found the marshal's office and entered. He assumed the white-haired man behind the desk was the lawman the bartender had been talking about.

"Howdy," the man said. "What can I do for you?"

"I just got to town," Clint said. "I heard Marshal Fredericks was a fair man."

"Well," the man said, sitting back in his chair, "been a while since somebody said somethin' nice about me. Who told you that?"

"Oh, somebody over at the Wild Mustang."

Fredericks laughed.

"I'm guessin' it wasn't the bartender, Ham," the lawman said. "He hates my guts."

"Ham?"

"Hamilton," Fredericks said, "folks call 'im Ham."

"Well, I talked to a bartender, don't know what his name was," Clint said, "but you're right, it wasn't him. Mind if I sit?"

"Be my guest."

Clint sat across from the man.

"What brings you to town?"

"I was passing by here yesterday, saw a bunch of men on horseback chasing a girl."

"The gypsy girl?" the lawman asked. "I heard about that. They said a band of gypsies chased them off, kept them from catching her. Lucky for her, I guess."

"Not so much," Clint said. "It wasn't a band of gypsies that sent them packing."

"Oh, who was it, then?"

Clint smiled at the man. "Just me."

Chapter Seventeen

"You," Marshal Fredericks said. "Alone, against six men?"

"I convinced them it wasn't in their best interest to go against me."

Fredericks smiled.

"And how did you do that?"

"I told them I'm Clint Adams."

Fredericks's smile broadened.

"And they believed you?" he asked. "That you're the Gunsmith?"

"They did."

"How did you pull that off?"

"Easy," Clint said. "I showed them."

"You . . . showed them?" Fredericks lost his smile. "You mean, you are the Gunsmith?"

"I am," Clint said.

"But . . . still . . . one against six?"

"None of them wanted to be the first one to die," Clint told him. "It's the same way you'd stand off a lynch mob, Marshal. You look like you've been in this business long enough to know that nobody wants to die first."

"Well . . . yeah, I know that." Fredericks squared his shoulders and tried to take control of the situation. "So what brings you to town, Mr. Adams?"

"I didn't like what those men were trying to do to a young girl," Clint said.

"A young gypsy girl," Fredericks pointed out.

"That makes no difference to me."

"Me, neither," the lawman said. "But most folks around here don't like gypsies. And did you hear what happened over in Silverton, Nevada?"

"I heard something," Clint said. "A rumor."

"That was no rumor. The sheriff there sent out a message to as many law enforcement officials as he could to be on the lookout for gypsies."

"Including you?"

"I got a telegram," Fredericks said.

"And you believe that gypsies burned the town down?" Clint asked.

"All I'm sayin' is that the word is out," Fredericks said.

"Well, that's no reason to hang a young girl," Clint pointed out. "Gypsy or not, that's not the kind of thing I'm going to look the other way for. Are you?"

"Of course not," Fredericks said. "But they're about to replace me here. They figure it's time for me to retire."

"Is that right?" Clint asked. "And who do they intend to put in your place?"

"They got a couple possibilities, both younger than me," the marshal said.

"And both of them *would* look the other way if a gypsy was about to be hanged, right?"

"That would be my bet," Fredericks said.

"Then I guess it would be wise for gypsies to stay out of Rock Springs."

"I think it'd be wise for gypsies to go back home," Fredericks said, "wherever they're from."

Clint stood up.

"How long will you be staying in town?" the marshal asked.

"I guess that depends."

"On what?"

"On whether or not this town tries to hang any young girls while I'm here."

He turned and left the office.

***

Lonny Shaye was walking across the street when he saw Clint Adams come out of the marshal's office. He quickly ducked into a doorway before the Gunsmith could see him.

He watched as Adams headed off down the street and didn't look back. When he was out of sight, Lonny stepped out and started off up the street in the opposite direction . . .

***

"Are you sure?" Ken Osborne asked Lonny.

"He shot my holster off my hip," Lonny said. "I think I'd know him when I saw him again. It was the Gunsmith."

Osborne was Lonny's boss, the owner of the Circle K ranch. He was a well-dressed man in his fifties, who used the Pretty Lady as his headquarters when he was in town. Also sitting at the table with them in The Pretty Lady Saloon was the foreman, Jim Drury. In his forties, he had been working for Osborne for over ten years, six of those as foreman.

"What the hell's he doin' in town?" Drury wondered aloud.

"He might be lookin' for me and the boys," Lonny said. "Maybe I should tell them to stay out of town."

"Don't go off half-cocked," Osborne said to Lonny in a soothing voice. "The fact is we don't know what he's doing here, so what we have to do is find out."

"And how do we do that?" Drury asked.

"Simple," Osborne said, "we ask."

"Adams?" Drury asked.

Osborne shook his head.

"The Marshal."

Chapter Eighteen

Marshal Fredericks came through the cell block door behind his desk and saw Ken Osborne standing there, with his foreman, Jim Drury.

"Gents," he said, putting aside the broom he was holding, "what can I do for you?"

"Do you mind if I sit, Marshal?" Osborne asked.

"Be my guest."

Osborne and Fredericks sat, with Drury standing behind his boss.

"We heard you had a visitor today," Osborne said.

"Since I've only had one," Fredericks said, "I can only assume you're talkin' about Clint Adams."

"The Gunsmith, right," Osborne said. "I want you to tell me what he wants. Why he's in town."

"He said he was passin' through," Fredericks lied.

"That's all?"

"That's what he said."

"Then he was lying," Osborne said, "or you are."

"Why would either of us lie?"

"I don't know," Osborne said. "Maybe he's here looking for someone."

"For what reason?"

"What reason does the Gunsmith ever have for finding someone?" Osborne asked. "To kill them."

"You're judging him by his reputation."

"What else do you judge a man like him by?" Drury asked.

"As far as I know," Fredericks said, "he's not here to kill anyone . . . in particular."

"So he says."

"Who do you think he'd want to kill?" Fredericks asked.

Osborne opened his mouth, as if to answer, but then shut it again.

"Who?" Fredericks asked.

"Never mind," Osborne said, standing up. "Forget we were ever here."

"Mr. Osborne—" the marshal started, but the rancher and hired foreman left the office. Fredericks wondered if he should warn Clint Adams.

***

"What happened?" Lonny asked, across the street from the marshal's office. "What'd you find out?"

"Nothing," Osborne said. "Either Adams was lying to the marshal, or Fredericks lied to us."

"What'd he say?" Lonny asked.

75

"That Adams ain't here to find and kill anybody," Drury answered.

"You sure somebody was lyin'?" Lonny asked. "Maybe he ain't lookin' for us."

"He said he's just passin' through," Drury answered.

"That could be true," Osborne said. "Jim, I want Lonny and the rest of the boys to go back to the ranch."

"Right, boss."

"That ain't fair," Lonny said. "We ain't been to town in so long."

"Then you shouldn't have wasted so much time chasing that gypsy girl," Osborne said.

"She stole from us!" Lonny said.

"Yeah," Drury said, sarcastically, "that's why you wanted her."

"I should've sent you back yesterday," Osborne said. "Now find the others and get out of town."

"Yes, Boss," Lonny said, and started away.

"What are we gonna do?" Drury asked.

"You go back with them," Osborne said, "and make sure they stay on the ranch."

"And you?"

"I'm going to have a conversation with Clint Adams," Osborne said.

"Why?"

"So I can decide for myself who's lying," Osborne said, "him or the marshal."

***

Marshal Fredericks gave Osborne and his foreman time to move on, then left his office. He realized he hadn't even asked Adams what hotel he was staying in, so he was just going to have to search the town for him. Hopefully, he'd find him before any of the hands from the Circle K did.

He tried the Wild Mustang Saloon first, where he talked to the bartender, Ham.

"Yeah, he was in here earlier," the man said, "but not since."

"Ham, this is important," Fredericks said. "If he comes in again, tell him I need to see him as soon as possible."

"Sure," Ham said, wiping an invisible puddle from the bar top with a rag, "I'll tell 'im, Marshal."

Chapter Nineteen

When Clint left the marshal's office, he knew he didn't have enough information to make his decision about whether or not to help the gypsies. Not yet, anyway. He figured he needed to find some of the men who were chasing her and get the whole story from them. He didn't know where the men from the Circle K did their drinking, so he was going to have to check all the saloons. He hit two before he found his way to The Pretty Lady.

"Yeah," the barkeep told him, "those boys drink here. They were here earlier, but now they're gone."

"Where?" Clint asked.

"The foreman and top hand came and dragged them back to the ranch."

"And where's that?"

"About five miles north of town. It's a big spread with a two story house and a big red barn. You can't miss it, but . . ."

"But what?"

"You may want to. Those boys are a rowdy bunch."

"How rowdy?"

The bartender, tall and not yet thirty, shifted his feet nervously and bit his lip.

"I think it's a little late to worry that you might've said too much."

"They tried to chase down a gypsy girl yesterday."

"I know," Clint said, "they were going to hang her. I stopped them."

"Hang her?" the bartender said. "Mister, they was gonna rape her!"

***

Fredericks couldn't be sure that Ham, the bartender, would give Clint Adams his message, so he just kept looking. He saw Adams coming out of The Pretty Lady from across the street and hurried over to him.

"I've been lookin' for you," he said.

"Why, Marshal?"

"Osborne, the owner of the Circle K, came to see me. He was askin' about you."

"Asking what?"

"Why you're here," Fredericks said.

"And what did you tell him?"

"Nothin'—" Fredericks said, "that is, I told him you said you were just passin' through."

"Did he believe you?"

"Maybe," Fredericks said. "He probably thought I was either lying to him, or you lied to me."

"But he sent his men back to his ranch."

"That doesn't surprise me. But I'm sure he's still here, lookin' for you."

"What for?" Clint asked. "Does he have a gun?"

"Yes, but it's not that," Fredericks said. "He wants to talk to you."

"That's fine with me," Clint said. "Where is he?"

"I don't know," the marshal said, "but pick a saloon. Either this one or the Wild Mustang, and he'll find you."

Clint looked back at the Pretty Lady, then said, "I'll go to the Mustang."

"I was there lookin' for you," Fredericks said, "left you a message with Ham. I don't know if he'll tell you."

"That's all right," Clint said. "I'll see you later, Marshal. Thanks for the warning."

"Let me know what happens," Fredericks said.

"I will," Clint promised.

"But do me a favor?"

"What's that?"

"Don't kill 'im."

"I won't if I don't have to."

They split up and went their separate ways.

***

Clint entered The Wild Mustang Saloon, found it crowded with activity. He made his way to the bar.

"Came back for a look at the girls, huh?" Ham, the bartender, asked.

"And another beer," Clint said.

"Comin' up."

As the bartender set it down Clint asked, "Have you seen Osborne, the rancher, tonight?"

"Nope, not here," Ham said, "but he usually drinks at The Pretty Lady."

"I heard he's looking for me."

"The marshal was here, he was lookin' for you," Ham said.

"He caught up with me," Clint said. "I guess I'll just stay around and give Osborne a chance to find me."

"He might have some of his men with him," Ham warned.

"From what I heard, he sent all of his men back to the ranch."

"Looks like you're right," Ham said.

"What do you mean?"

"He just walked in," the bartender said, "and he's alone."

Chapter Twenty

Clint turned and watched the large, older man approach him.

"Adams?"

"Are you Mr. Osborne?" Clint asked.

"I am."

"I hear you've been looking for me."

"I want to talk," Osborne said. "Can we sit?"

"Sure," Clint said, "if we can find a table."

Osborne looked at Ham.

"Can we use your back room?"

"Sure," Ham said, "there's no game goin' on there right now."

"Let me have a beer," Osborne said.

Ham put one on the bar for him. Osborne picked it up and turned to Clint.

"Ready?" he asked.

"Lead the way."

Clint carried his own beer and followed Osborne across the crowded floor to a curtained doorway.

There was a large, round poker table in the room, with six chairs. They each sat.

"I've heard from the marshal that you're just passing through."

"Well," Clint said, "that's what I told him."

"Ah, but it was a lie."

"Not exactly."

"Are you after my men?"

"You mean the men who were chasing a gypsy girl to rape her?"

"They weren't going to rape her," Osborne said. "She stole from them."

"Did she steal from you?"

"Not exactly."

"Have you had experiences with other gypsies?" Clint asked.

"I have, and not good ones," Osborne said, "They lie, cheat and steal."

"All of them?"

"It's what they do, Adams," Osborne said. "None of them are different."

"Do you know the girl's people?"

"No," Osborne said, "I know she came to town alone, ran into my men and then . . . something happened. She stole from them."

"That's what they told you?"

"Yes."

"And you believed them?"

"Over the word of a gypsy girl?" Osborne asked. "Yes."

"Then they can tell you anything and you'll believe them," Clint said, "if it has to do with gypsies."

Osborne frowned.

"If I find out any of my men are lying to me, they're fired."

"I'd like to know that, too," Clint said.

"And if I find out you're lying to me," Osborne went on, "or the marshal lied to me—"

"I told the marshal I wasn't here to kill any of your men," Clint said, "and I meant it. But that doesn't mean I won't if they come after me."

Osborne drank half his beer and stood up.

"I'll make sure that doesn't happen."

"Then we won't have a problem with each other," Clint said. "But can you tell me what would happen if a band of gypsies showed up around here?"

"Nothing good," Osborne said. "Even if I keep my men at bay, there are others in town who hate gypsies. We all read in the newspaper what happened in Silverton."

"So as long as people think it was gypsies who burned down that town . . ."

". . . there'd be a problem if they showed up here."

"And what if it's not the same band?"

"I don't think anybody will care," Osborne said. "I'm heading back to my ranch to talk to my men. Will you still be around tomorrow?"

"I believe so."

"Then maybe I'll see you then."

Osborne turned and left the saloon.

Clint picked up his beer and carried it to the bar.

"That didn't look too bad," Ham said.

"He seems to be a reasonable man."

"When it suits him," Ham said.

"I suppose you could say that about anybody," Clint commented.

***

Osborne headed directly for the livery stable from the saloon. As he approached, someone stepped out of an alley, grabbed him from behind and dragged him in. Once there, they produced a knife and drew the blade across his throat. Blood poured down the front of his shirt. The killer released him, and Osborne slumped to the ground, dead.

Chapter Twenty-One

The knocking woke Clint the next morning. He grabbed his gun and staggered to the door.

"Who is it?"

"Marshal Fredericks."

Clint opened the door a crack.

"What can I do for you?"

"Can I come in? Don't worry, I'm alone."

"Sure."

Clint opened the door, took a quick look into the hall to be sure the marshal was alone.

"Come on in."

He walked to the bed and sat down, still holding his gun. He was wearing only his underwear.

"You mind if I get dressed while we talk?" he asked, reaching for his pants.

"No problem," Fredericks said. "I won't take long."

Clint holstered his gun and started to pull on his trousers. He kept an alert eye on the lawman, in case he started to draw his gun.

"You did talk to Osborne last night, didn't you?"

"I did," Clint said, "for a short time."

"In the Mustang?"

Clint stood up, looked around for his shirt.

"That's right."

"Then what?"

"Then I came here."

"Do you know where he went?"

"I assumed he went back to his ranch." He slipped on his shirt. "What's this about, Marshal?"

"He's dead."

"What?"

"His body was found in an alley this morning," Fredericks said. "His throat was cut."

"Any idea who did it?"

"The word's already going around town," Fredericks said. "Gypsies."

"Anybody who wanted him dead would know the gypsies would be blamed, especially if he was killed with a knife."

"I know that."

"Then why are you here?" Clint said. "To ask me if I did it?"

"I don't think you did it," Fredericks said. "Not with a knife, anyway."

"Then what do you need from me?" Clint asked, sitting down to pull on his boots.

"The girl you saved from Osborne's men," Fredericks said. "What did you do with her?"

"I took her to her people."

"Can you tell me where they are?"

"I can tell you where they were," Clint said. "They've probably moved on by now."

"That's okay," Fredericks said. "I'd just have to track them from there."

"Taking a posse out?" Clint asked.

"Not right away," Fredericks said. "I just wanna talk to them."

"How good are you at tracking?"

"It's not my specialty," the marshal said, "but if there are a few wagons, it shouldn't be too hard to follow their trail."

"I could come with you," Clint offered.

"Why would you do that?"

"To make sure you find them," Clint said, "and that you're alone when you do. And to make sure they're safe, for now."

"Do you think I'd lie to you and take a posse out there?" Fredericks asked.

"I don't know," Clint said. "Would you?"

"I can be ready to go in an hour," Fredericks said.

"Good, that gives me time for breakfast," Clint said. "I'll meet you out front."

***

Clint still wasn't sure he could trust the marshal, so he was very careful when he walked Eclipse over to the hotel after breakfast. Just in case Fredericks wasn't alone.

He got there before the marshal, who appeared about fifteen minutes later, walking a good-looking Shetland pony.

"Handsome animal," Clint said.

"Thanks," Fredericks said. "I only hope he can keep up with yours."

The Shetland wasn't as big as Eclipse, and had shorter legs, but from the looks of him, Clint felt sure the pony would do fine.

"Let's go?" Clint said.

"Yeah," Fredericks said, mounting up. "I want to get out of town before Osborne's men show up."

"You think they're on their way?" Clint asked, also mounting.

"Take my word for it," Fredericks said. "They'll be on their way as soon as they hear the news."

Chapter Twenty-Two

They managed to get a few miles away from town before they ran into a group of riders heading their way.

"Is that them?" Clint asked.

"Gotta be."

"It's not your posse, is it?" Clint asked.

"No posse, Adams," Fredericks said. "I told you that. They must've got the word pretty early this morning."

They reined in and waited for the riders to reach them. When they all reined in their horses and sat there in a cloud of dust, Clint recognized a couple from the incident with Ayesha.

"Drury," Fredericks said, "this is Clint Adams. Mr. Adams, Jim Drury, the foreman of the Circle K."

"And I recognize a couple of these men," Clint said.

"Yeah," Drury said, "you crossed paths with Lonny and Sam before, kept them from taking care of a girl who stole from them."

"Kept them from raping a young girl, you mean," Clint said.

"A gypsy girl," Drury said. "What else would she be good for?"

"Where are you headed, Jim?" Fredericks asked.

"We were on our way to town, Marshal," the foreman said. "We heard our boss was killed last night. But since you're here, we'll just ask you . . . is that right?"

"It is," Fredericks said. "He's dead, killed in an alley last night."

The eight men riding with the foreman all shifted in their saddles.

"What are you gonna do about it?" Drury asked.

"Whataya think?" Fredericks said. "I'm gonna do my job, find out who did it and arrest 'em."

"Find out?" Drury said. "You already know who did it. We heard his throat was cut."

"You heard right."

"That makes it a gypsy," Drury said. "You know that as well as I do."

"Unfortunately," Fredericks said, "there are no gypsies in town, and there were none last night."

"You don't know that," Lonny spoke up. "They're sneaks. They could be there and you ain't seen 'em."

"Where are you headed now?" Drury asked. "With him." He motioned toward Clint.

"Just gonna check out a lead," Fredericks said.

"We'll come with ya," Drury said. "You might need our help with that girl's people."

"I don't think so," Fredericks said. "I think you boys better get back to town and take care of your boss's body. He's at the undertaker's."

"He ain't goin' nowhere," Drury said. "We'll come with you."

"I said no."

"You gonna stop us, old timer?" Drury asked.

"He is," Clint said, "with my help."

Drury looked at Clint.

"You managed to back down six of my men the other day," he said, "but I wasn't with them, and I got eight now."

"There's nine of you," Clint said. "I can count. But if anybody goes for a gun, I'll kill you first. That's a promise, Mr. Drury."

"And you'd go along with that?" Drury asked the lawman.

"If you interfere with my business, you're interferin' with the law," Fredericks said, "so yeah, I'd back his play. I'm sure I could get at least one of you before you got me."

"And I bet I could get a few more," Clint said. "Is that going to be worth it to you? You think your men want to take the risk that they'll be among the ones we get?"

Now it was the foreman's turn to shift in his saddle, take a look at his men. Then he turned back to Clint and Fredericks.

"We'll be in town, then," he said. "Waitin' for ya."

"I got no problem with that," Fredericks said. "Take care of your boss. We'll be back soon."

Clint started Eclipse forward, followed by Fredericks and his Shetland. The men from the Circle K split into two groups and allowed them to pass, then they continued on their way to town.

Clint and Fredericks stopped and watched them ride off.

"Think they'll try to follow us?" Clint asked.

"I'm pretty sure we can keep that from happenin'," Fredericks said.

"And what'll happen when we get back to town?" Clint asked.

"That'll depend on whether or not we ride in with any gypsies."

"I thought we were just going to talk to them, if we find them," Clint said.

"That's the plan."

"Glad to hear it."

They turned their horses and started off again.

"You know," Fredericks said, "by the time we get back to town, Drury could have more than eight men backin' him."

"That's okay," Clint said, "I've got another gun in my saddle bag."

Chapter Twenty-Three

After they left Clint Adams and the marshal, the men of the Circle K rode toward town. But once they were out of sight of the two men, Drury put his hand up to stop their progress.

"What's up, boss?" Lonny asked.

"You take the men to town," Drury told him. "Check on the boss's body at the undertaker's and make arrangements for him to be brought out to the ranch."

"The ranch?" Lonny asked. "Not boot hill?"

"He'd want to be buried on his ranch," Drury said, "so that's what we're gonna do."

"All right," Lonny said, "but where are you goin'?"

"I'm gonna track Adams and the lawman," Drury said. "I wanna see where they're goin'."

"Make sure they don't see ya," Lonny said.

"I'm not gonna follow them," Drury said, "I'm gonna follow their tracks. There's no way they *can* see me."

"Why not take a few men with ya?" Lonny asked.

"No," Drury said, "that's one way they might see me. No, I'll go alone. I'm just lookin' this time. I ain't gonna do nothin'—not until later. I'll meet you and the boys back at the ranch."

"Sure, boss," Lonny said.

"Lonny and the men watched as Drury rode back the way they had come, then turned and continued on to town.

***

"This is it," Clint said, looking around.

"Are you sure?"

"You can see where the wagons were," Clint said, "and the fires."

"So where are they now?"

"They went there," Clint said, pointing, "and there . . . and there."

"What are you sayin'?"

"They've split up."

"Why?"

"Probably so nobody could catch them all together."

"But why would they do that, unless they did somethin' they don't wanna get caught for."

"Like murder?"

"What else?"

"Try stealing."

"That, too," Fredericks said.

"Like you said, these wagon tracks will be easy to follow," Clint said. "Do you want to take one set, and I'll take another?"

"Who's in charge of this band?" Fredericks asked.

"King Milosh."

"King?" the marshal asked. "A real King?"

"So they say."

"Then he's the one I should talk to," Fredericks said. "Wouldn't you agree?"

"If all you want to do is talk, then yeah, I'd say so," Clint agreed.

"But the question is, which of these wagon tracks would lead us to him?"

Clint studied the tracks. The wagon that he had spent the night with Varna in was the largest, so the biggest, deepest tracks would belong to that one. The rest of the wagons were the same size.

"There's no way to tell," Clint said. "But I have an idea that even though they split up and went in different directions, they're probably all going to the same place."

"So we only need to follow one," Fredericks said, "together."

"That makes sense," Clint said.

The two men looked at each other, then mounted their horses and started to follow the larger, deeper, easiest trail.

***

When they came within sight of the large wagon, it was sitting in a field alone, with no one around it.

"What the hell—" Fredericks said. "Did they just leave it there?"

"Could be somebody inside," Clint said. "Could be they're the first ones to arrive."

Fredericks looked around.

"Could this be a trap?" he asked. "Maybe they're watchin' and waitin' for us."

"How would they know we were coming?" Clint asked.

"They'd know if they killed Osborne," Marshal Fredericks pointed out.

"If they killed Osborne," Clint said, "I doubt they'd wait around for the law to find them."

Fredericks reached out and grabbed Clint's arm.

"What if they're in town?" he asked. "What if they're gonna burn it down?"

"Take it easy, Marshal," Clint said. "Let's go one step at a time. First, let's have a look at the wagon."

Clint started to slowly ride toward it, followed cautiously by Marshal Fredericks.

Chapter Twenty-Four

"Stay mounted," Clint told Fredericks. "I'll have a look inside."

He dismounted from Eclipse and walked to the wagon.

"Hello the wagon," he called. "Anyone inside?"

There was no answer.

"I'm coming in," he said, and pulled the flap to the side. As he stuck his head in, Varna looked at him and smiled.

"I've been expecting you," she said. The interior was filled with the aroma of her readiness. Under other circumstances, that and her naked breasts and nipples would have made his mouth water. In fact, he felt his body responding to her in spite of the marshal's presence. He was almost dizzy but managed to shake it off.

He helplessly ran his eyes up and down her naked form but said, "I can see that. But I'm thinking you better get dressed."

She pouted and asked, "Why's that?"

"I'm not alone."

She grabbed her clothes and held them in front of her naked body.

"Who is with you?"

"The marshal of Rock Springs."

"Why?"

"There was a murder in town," Clint said. "He wants to talk to somebody from your gypsy band. I told him it should be Milosh, but you're the only one here."

"I will get dressed and come out."

"All right," he said. "I'll give you some privacy."

He stepped back and let the flap fall closed as she started to move around.

"Everythin' all right?" Fredericks called.

"Yes," Clint said "there was someone inside. She's coming out to talk."

Fredericks looked around, before dismounting.

"The King isn't here?" he asked.

"No one's here except Varna," Clint said. "But she'll have all the answers you want."

They waited until Varna was ready to step down. When she moved the flap aside Clint went to the wagon, put both hands on her waist and helped her down.

"Varna, this is Marshal Fredericks, from Rock Springs."

"Hello," she said, "I am Varna."

Fredericks stared at the beauty before him, his mouth slightly open.

"Marshal?" Clint said.

"Huh? What?"

"You said you had some questions for Varna," Clint reminded him.

"Oh, yeah . . . where are all your people? Why have they left you alone? Are you all right?"

Clint could see that Fredericks was immediately smitten with the gypsy beauty.

"Yes, I am fine," she said. "The others will be here soon."

"Does that include your King?" Fredericks looked at Clint for help.

"Milosh."

"Yeah, that's it, King Milosh," Fredericks said.

"I am sure he will be here."

"Why don't I make a fire for you while we wait," Clint suggested,

"Thank you," she said, "that would be very nice."

"I'll help!" Fredericks said, anxiously.

The lawman and Clint collected firewood, then started the flame so that Varna could put on a pot of gypsy tea.

"Tea?" Fredericks said, looking at Clint.

"It's more potent than any tea you've had before," Clint assured him.

Eventually, they were gathered around the fire, each with a cup of tea.

"Marshal, you have some questions for me?" Varna asked. "Clint told me there was a murder in town."

"Yeah," Fredericks said, "a rancher named Osborne."

"I don't know the name," she said. "Is it someone we should know?"

"Clint told me he saved a young gypsy girl from some men the other day," Fredericks said.

"Yes," Varna said, "that was our Ayesha."

"Well, those men were ranch hands who worked for Mr. Osborne."

"I am sorry," she said, "do you think Ayesha killed this man? She is very young, and—"

"No, no," Fredericks said, "I'm sure the girl didn't do it, just as I'm sure you didn't."

"That's very nice of you," she said.

"But he was killed with a knife," Fredericks said, "his throat cut. It could've been one of your men, looking for revenge."

"But you said Clint saved her from those men," Varna said, looking confused. "So what would there be to avenge?"

"Miss Varna—"

"Just Varna," she said.

"—I'm afraid the ranch hands from the Circle K may come looking for you and your people."

"Then you have come to warn us?"

"Yeah, that's it," Fredericks said, "I wanna warn you."

"I will tell King Milosh you were kind enough to do that, Marshal."

Fredericks stood up. Varna did the same, accepting the cup from him, noticing that he had consumed very little of the tea. Clint stood and handed her his cup, empty.

"Would you like to stay and wait for the rest of my people?" she asked. "King Milosh would like me to invite you to eat with us."

"No," the marshal said, "I have to get back to town."

"Then perhaps another time," she said.

"Yeah," Fredericks said, "another time."

He and Clint walked to their horses and mounted up.

"Do you see him?" Clint asked.

"No," Fredericks said, "who?"

"Somebody's watching us."

"One rider?"

"Yes."

"Could it be the King?"

"No," Clint said, "I think it's one of the Osborne boys, maybe even the foreman."

"Where is he?"

"Never mind," Clint said. "I don't want you to look."

They both waved at Varna and turned their horses to ride away.

"Do you think she'll be all right alone?" Fredericks asked.

"She'll be fine."

"She's a real beauty," the lawman said.

"Yes," Clint agreed, "that she is."

Chapter Twenty-Five

"Should we double back and grab 'im?" Fredericks asked.

"What for?"

"He might be threatening Varna."

"He's right behind us," Clint said.

"How come you didn't notice him when he was following us before?"

"Because he wasn't following us, he was tracking us," Clint said. "He stayed back far enough to go unseen."

"But not now," Fredericks said.

"No, now he's either being stupid," Clint said, "or he wants us to see him."

"So what do we do?" the lawman asked.

"Let's just let him follow us back to town," Clint said. "We can talk to him there."

They rode in silence for a few miles and then Fredericks said, "We didn't find out very much, did we?"

"Nothing helpful," Clint said. "Whether a gypsy did it or not, they'd say they didn't, but that pretty much goes for anybody."

"If a gypsy killed him, folks will figure it was because he's a gypsy," Fredericks said. "If somebody else did it, then . . . why?"

"It sounds like Osborne was a successful rancher," Clint said. "Didn't he have any enemies?"

"I'm sure he had a few, but nobody who'd wanna kill 'im," the marshal said.

"What about his men?" Clint asked. "Or maybe he fired somebody, recently."

"You'd have to ask the foreman about that," Fredericks said, "and according to you, he's right behind us."

"Yeah, we can do that later," Clint said. "When we get back to town."

***

After the two men left, Varna dumped the remainder of her tea into the fire and went back to the wagon. Both Milosh and Ethelinda had assured her that the curse the old woman cast would bring Clint Adams back to her. That was the only reason she had waited for him, naked. When he showed up with the local marshal, it was a total surprise, and one Varna didn't like. The lawman had obviously swooned over her, but once again Clint Adams seemed unaffected by her.

Both Milosh and Ethelinda were going to have a lot of explaining to do.

***

Each man rode the remainder of the way deep in thought. Fredericks was wondering what to do next, how to go about finding out who killed Osborne. He was a town marshal, not a damned detective.

Clint was wondering about the gypsies, and how Varna was so sure he'd find her in the wagon that she waited for him naked? She must have really thought Clint had become obsessed with her. If that was the case, she was only due for disappointment. He liked her and had enjoyed their night together. It had been a long time since Clint had been obsessed with a single woman. He considered himself too old and jaded for something like that to happen again.

They took their horses to the livery, then stopped just outside.

"Where are you off to?" Clint asked.

"The undertaker," the lawman said. "I've got to see if those men took care of Mr. Osborne or not. How about you?"

"The Wild Mustang," Clint said. "I want a beer to wash the taste of that tea from my mouth."

"Not a bad idea," Fredericks said, "I'll join you after the undertaker."

"See you there."

Chapter Twenty-Six

During his walk from the livery to the Wild Mustang Saloon, Clint did not see hide nor hair of the foreman, Drury. He hoped the man hadn't doubled back to approach Varna.

When he entered the saloon, it was early evening. He and the marshal had been out most of the afternoon.

"Beer?" Ham asked, as he stepped to the bar.

"Yeah, a big, cold one."

"Only kind I serve."

Ham set the beer down in front of him. There were men on either side of Clint, but they gave him plenty of elbow room.

"The marshal find you?"

"I found him."

"So you know about Osborne?" Ham asked.

"I heard. Have you seen his men?"

"They been in town," Ham said. "Most of them are in the Pretty Lady drinkin' to their boss."

They were probably there waiting the return of their foreman, Drury.

"The bartender at the Pretty Lady warned me that the Circle K boys were a rowdy bunch."

"They are."

"How rowdy?" Clint asked.

"What do you mean?"

"What would they do to avenge their boss's death?"

Ham shrugged.

"Anythin'."

"If they believe he was killed by a gypsy—"

"—and if they get drunk enough, they'd kill a band of gypsies. Any band they could find."

"That's what I was afraid of," Clint said.

He was going to have to warn Milosh and Varna, and their band, not to stay where he found Varna. Drury, the foreman, knew they were there.

"Thanks," he said, draining the beer and leaving the saloon.

***

Drury entered the Pretty Lady, found all his men there among the other customers, except for his top hand.

"Where's Lonny?" he asked one of the other men.

"He's upstairs with one of the girls, boss," the man replied.

"Which girl?"

The man turned and asked the bartender, then said, "Crystal, room five."

Drury went up the steps, found room five and opened the door without knocking. Lonny was busily plunging his cock into the depths of a long-legged blonde. Her limbs were wrapped around his waist and she was able to see Drury over Lonny's shoulder. Her eyes widened and she beat her right fist on Lonny's back, trying to bring Drury's appearance to his attention. But Lonny was hastily driving himself to his completion, and it was only Drury's voice that brought him out of it.

"Lonny! Goddamnit!"

The younger man seemed to awaken from his trance. He withdrew from Crystal, who hastily covered herself— though not before Drury could see the corn silk hair between her thighs.

"Boss!" Lonny said, turning in bed so that his long erection pointed toward the door.

"Cover that up!" Drury said, looking away.

"Oh, sorry, boss," Lonny said, grabbing the sheet. He covered himself and at the same time uncovered Crystal. She put one hand down between her legs and tried to cover her small, pointy breasts with her other arm.

"I was jus' tryin' ta kill time til you got back, boss," Lonny said. "Where ya been?"

"I found them."

"Them? Who?"

"The gypsies."

"The one who killed the boss?" Lonny asked.

"What does it matter?" Drury asked. "They're gypsies."

"So what are we gonna do?" Lonny asked.

"We're gonna bury the boss tomorrow," Drury said, "and then take care of them."

"Kill 'em?" Lonny asked.

Drury nodded, then looked at the naked girl.

"Go downstairs and get me a whiskey!" he told her. As she hastily donned her dress, he looked at Lonny. "Get dressed and get out. When she comes back up, she's mine."

"Sure thing, boss," Lonny said, grabbing his pants. "Sure thing."

***

King Milosh's wagon was the next to last one to arrive safely. Varna watched as Milosh dropped down from the wagon and approached the fire.

"Did he come?" Milosh asked Varna.

"He did."

"And?"

"He brought the marshal with him."

"Is he going to help us?"

"We didn't have time to discuss that," she told him.

"Then what happened?"

She handed her King a cup of tea.

"There was a murder in town," she said. "A man named Osborne."

"He owns the ranch those men work on," Milosh said.

"Yes."

"Who killed him?"

"They don't know."

"Then the people in town will assume we did it," Milosh concluded.

"No doubt," Varna said.

"We will have to move on," Milosh said. "We have no choice."

"No, we do not," Varna agreed.

"All right," he said. "Has everyone arrived?"

"No."

"How many are missing?" he asked.

"Just one."

"Who is it?"

"Ayesha."

"What?"

"I'm sorry, Milosh," Varna said. "She is not here."

"Find out if anyone saw her," he ordered.

"Milosh," she responded, "you said we have to go."

"I am not leaving without my daughter."

"She's not really your daughter," Varna reminded him.

"I know that!" he said. "Do it."

"Yes, my King."

Milosh took out his whiskey flask and poured a healthy dollop into his tea.

Chapter Twenty-Seven

Clint found the marshal in his office.

"I was just comin' over to join you at the Mustang."

"I had another idea," Clint said.

"What's that?"

"Let's get a drink at the Pretty Lady."

***

"Drink up!" Drury shouted to his men. "We're headin' back to the Circle K."

They all drained their glasses, but as they turned to leave, Clint and Marshal Fredericks entered. They stopped just inside the batwing doors.

"Glad you fellas are still here," Fredericks said.

"We were just leavin'," Drury said.

"Headed where?" Clint asked.

"We're takin' the boss's body back to the ranch," Drury said. "He'd wanna be buried there."

"Why not stay for one more drink?" Clint suggested.

"It'll be dark soon."

"It won't take long," Clint said. "We have to talk. I tell you what, go ahead and send your men."

Drury studied Clint for a moment, then looked at Lonny and said, "Take the men and get back to the ranch."

"Whatever you say, boss." Lonny led the Circle K boys out of the saloon.

"Why don't you two get a table," Clint said. "I'll get the beers."

Clint went to the bar, collected three cold beers from the bartender, then carried them to the table the other two had staked out.

"What's on your mind?" Drury asked, as Clint sat down.

"That's the question on my mind," Clint said. "You tracked us today, then followed us back. What's on your mind?"

"Right now all I'm thinkin' about is buryin' my boss," Drury said.

"And then what?" Clint asked.

"What're you gettin' at?" Drury asked.

"Gypsies," Clint said, "I'm gettin' at gypsies. Now that you think you know where they are, what are you plannin'?"

"Come on, Drury," Fredericks said. "You and your men are known to be hotheads."

"Get to your point, Marshal," Drury said.

"The point is," Clint said, before the marshal could answer, "we don't want you going off half-cocked and after those gypsies. The fact is, nobody knows who killed your boss."

"Maybe *you* don't," Drury said, "but we have a pretty good idea."

"That's what we're talkin' about, Drury," Fredericks said. "Just because you think you know who killed him—"

"Look," Drury said, standing quickly and cutting the man off, "I get it, you don't want us killin' gypsies. Well then, why don't you tell the gypsies to stay away and not kill any of us? And by the way, not to steal from us, either."

"That's fair," Clint said, "but like I said before, if I catch any of your men trying to rape young gypsy girls—"

"You got no proof that was what they were gonna do!" Drury snapped.

"And you've got no proof a gypsy killed your boss," Clint said.

"You wanna avoid trouble?" Drury said to them. "Then go and find out who did kill 'im."

He turned and stormed out of the saloon.

"There's gonna be trouble," Fredericks said.

"Unless, like he said, you find the killer," Clint pointed out.

"I don't know what the chances of that are," Fredericks said. "I'm no detective."

"Well, I can't tell you who did it, but I can tell you I don't think it was a gypsy."

"Then who do you think it was?"

"I don't know the people of this town like you do," Clint said, "so I can't answer that question. I'm afraid you're on your own, Marshal."

Clint left the Pretty Lady and headed for his hotel.

***

The look on the face of the young desk clerk as he entered the lobby was a dead giveaway.

"Any messages?" he asked, stopping at the desk.

"Uh, no, sir."

"Got anything to tell me?"

"Uh, no sir." The clerk's voice squeaked that time.

"Is there somebody in my room?"

"Uh . . . excuse me, sir?" the clerk said, his eyes wide and watery.

"It better not be somebody with a gun," Clint said.

"Oh, no sir," the clerk said, "I would never—"

"I hope not," Clint said, "because I'll be back."

Clint went to his room, fairly certain from the clerk's attitude that whoever was waiting by his room didn't have a gun.

Chapter Twenty-Eight

He stopped in front of his door, put his right hand on his gun, unlocked the door with his left and entered. The girl was sitting on the bed with her hands folded in her lap.

"Aren't your people going to miss you, Ayesha?" he asked, closing the door.

"They're not my people," she said.

"We're talking about the gypsies, right?" Clint asked. "King Milosh's people?"

"Yes."

"What do you mean, they're not your people?" he asked. "I thought Milosh was your father."

She looked down at her hands.

"I was stolen," she said.

"The gypsies stole you?"

"Yes," she said, "well, no. They say they rescued me."

He walked to the bed and sat down next to her.

"When?"

"Seventeen years ago."

"Seven . . . you mean you were stolen as a baby?" he asked.

"Rescued," she said. "They told me I was about two years old."

"I thought gypsies stealing babies was a myth."

"I keep telling you," she insisted, "they didn't steal me, they rescued me."

"Yes, you've said that several times," Clint said. "Why don't you tell me about it?"

"It was in New York City," she said. "I was with my mother and father one day. My father, apparently, was a brute. I remember he was yelling at my mother, hitting her, right there on the street while people watched. And then he hit me. That's when the gypsies stepped in. King Milosh said they couldn't leave me with such a man."

"So they grabbed you."

"Yes, he and Varna. They took me to their people, and we left New York the next day."

"And you've been living with them ever since."

"Yes."

"But you don't consider them your people."

"Well, I do," she said, "but they're really not."

"And here I was wondering why you don't look like a gypsy."

"I know," she said, touching her hair, "I'm too fair."

"Is that why they were testing your ability to steal?" he asked.

"Yes," she said, "you see, I'm coming of age."

"To steal?"

"Yes."

"Ayesha," he asked, "why are you here?"

She turned her head and looked at him.

"I need your help."

"Why?"

"King Milosh and Varna," she said, "they are going to sell me back to my father."

"I don't understand," Clint said. "When did all of this happen?"

"They told me last night."

"They told you?"

"Well . . . I heard them talking."

"What did they say, exactly?"

"They said my real father was rich, and he wants me back, so they're going to sell me to him."

"That's it?"

"I—I don't remember everything," she said.

"Well," Clint said, "how about you tell me what you do remember."

She hesitated, then started speaking.

"They said they had to give me back, because they didn't want the same thing to happen here that happened in Silverton."

"Silverton?" he asked. "Ayesha, Silverton burned down. Did Milosh and his people do that?"

"No," she said.

"Do you know who did?"

She shrugged and said, "No."

"Ayesha—"

"King Milosh thinks my father did it," she said. "He thinks my father burned down the town to . . . he said to make a point."

"Jesus," Clint said, "who's your father?"

"He's a rich man from back East," she said. "That's all I know."

"And you were stolen from him when you were . . . what? Two years old?"

"I guess."

"And he wants you back now?" Clint asked. "Why?"

"I—I don't know."

"Have you talked to Milosh and Varna about this?"

"No."

"Why not?"

"They didn't know I was listening," she said. "When Milosh said we all had to leave camp separately, and meet later, I . . . I left."

"And came here?"

"I . . . I didn't know where to go," she said. "I don't want them to send me back. You were the only one I could think of to come to."

"Well, all right," Clint said. "Why don't you sleep here tonight, and in the morning we'll figure out what to do."

"A-all right."

"You take the bed."

"What about you?"

"I'll be fine," he said. "I'll sit in the chair."

"No," she said, "we can share the bed."

"Ayesha," he said, "we've been through this. You're very young—"

"I don't want to be alone," she said. "We could just lie together and stay dressed."

He studied her face for a few moments. She looked scared, lonely and confused.

"All right," he said. "But let's take off our boots."

They both did that. He hung his gunbelt on the bedpost, then got under the covers with her. She cuddled against him, putting her head on his shoulder. He could feel the heat of her firm, young body right through their clothes, but he wasn't about to take advantage of her.

"Good-night. Clint," she said, "thank you."

In moments, she was asleep. It took him a bit longer.

Chapter Twenty-Nine

In the morning Clint told Ayesha he was taking her to breakfast.

"The people in town . . ." she said, warningly.

"You'd be recognized by men from the Circle K," he said, "but maybe not the folks in town. We've already agreed that you don't really look like a gypsy."

He wanted to talk to her over a nice, calm breakfast, so he simply took her to the hotel dining room.

"Okay," he said, once they were eating, "here's what I want to do. I want to go and talk to Milosh about you."

"I can't go back!" she said.

"You stay here, in my hotel room, until I come back," he said. "Don't go out alone. All right?"

"Yes," she said. "Thank you."

"Do you trust Milosh?" he asked.

"No."

"Do you trust Varna?"

She hesitated, then said, "Yes."

"Okay, so maybe I'll talk to her."

"Yes," Ayesha said, "that would be good."

"Then it's agreed," he said. "I'll talk to Varna, find out what's going on."

"Yes."

"And then there's another thing."

"What?" she asked, chewing her bacon.

"A man was killed yesterday," Clint said. "Mr. Osborne, the rancher those men who chased you work for. Do you know anything about that?"

Her eyes got wide and she said, "No."

"His throat was cut."

"That's terrible."

"Folks around here think it was a gypsy."

"I don't think it was any of us," she said.

"All right. Ayesha, do you know your father's name? The man Milosh took you away from?"

"No."

"Does Milosh know?"

"I think so," she said. "He must—but I—I'm not sure."

"That's something else I can ask Varna."

"Be careful," she said.

"Of who?"

"The gypsies."

"What do you mean?"

"Ethelinda," she said, "she can cast spells."

"Ethelinda?"

"The old woman."

"Ah, an old gypsy woman who can cast spells."

"Yes," Ayesha said. "It's real, not funny."

125

"I'm sorry," Clint said. "Is there anyone else there who can cast spells?"

"Well . . ."

"Yes?"

"Varna."

"What kind of spells can she cast?"

"Love spells," Ayesha said. "She can make men fall in love with her."

"I see."

"Are you?"

"Am I what?"

"In love with her."

"No, I'm not."

"Then her spell didn't work on you."

"And the old woman," he said. "Ethelinda? Who is she going to cast a spell on?"

"On you . . . I think."

"What kind of spell?"

"I don't know."

Ayesha didn't seem to know a lot, just enough to be scared and confused.

"All right," he said. "I'll take you back to my room, then ride out to see Varna."

"Be careful of King Milosh," she said.

"Is he dangerous?" Clint asked.

"He can be."

"Then I'll be careful," he said. "Come on . . ."

Chapter Thirty

Clint left Ayesha in his room and rode out to where he had last seen Varna and her wagon. He was hoping the other gypsies would still be there, and that they hadn't moved on yet. For one thing, he'd be able to warn them about the Circle K boys. And for another, he'd be able to talk to Varna, and maybe to King Milosh, and find out what was going on with Ayesha.

When he came within sight of the clearing, he saw all the wagons gathered there. He looked around, and there was no sign of any other riders. So far, so good . . .

He rode up to the camp and the people stood around, waiting to greet him. As he dismounted, Milosh and Varna stepped forward.

"Do you know where she is?" Milosh asked.

"Who?" Clint said.

"Ayesha," the King said. "You are the only one she would go to."

"Actually, I do know."

"Is she all right?" Varna asked.

"She's fine," Clint said. "Just a little scared and confused."

"Why?" Milosh asked.

"Because she doesn't want you to send her back."

Varna looked at Milosh quickly.

"Back where?" he asked, ignoring her look.

"I think you know that better than I do, Milosh."

"Let us take care of your horse and we can sit and talk," the King said.

"My horse is fine right here," Clint assured him, "but yes, let's talk."

"Come to the fire," Milosh said.

Clint followed Milosh and Varna to the fire.

"Tea?" Varna offered.

"No, thank you," Clint said. "I haven't acquired a taste for that."

"Coffee, then?" she asked.

"Yes, please."

She handed him a cup and then hunkered down at the fire with both of them.

"What did Ayesha tell you?" Milosh asked.

"Just what she heard you and Varna talking about," Clint said. "That her real father wants her back, and you're going to sell her."

Varna's hand went to her mouth. Clint looked around, saw men, women and children watching them. He wondered if any of the older women he could see was Ethelinda.

"Is it true, what she told me?" Clint asked. "You stole her—rescued her—when she was small, took her from her family?"

"We were in New York, trying to earn enough money to start west," Milosh said. "And yes, we were on the street, picking pockets, when we saw a man beating his wife, with a small child standing there watching. Then he struck the child . . . and at that moment, I took her."

"Without anyone seeing you?"

"Yes," Milosh said. "The man had gone back to beating his wife, and people were watching them, so I took her."

"And headed west."

"And raised her as my own," Milosh said. "My own wife and child had died of a plague before we left Hungary. This was my chance to have a daughter."

"So what's this talk about giving her back?" Clint asked. "How could the man have found her after all these years?"

"He is very wealthy, and he hired many detectives," Milosh said.

"And what about Silverton?" Clint asked.

"That was where they found us, right near that town," Milosh said. "I refused to give Ayesha to him, so he decided to make an example."

"By burning Silverton down?"

"His men did," Milosh said. "He was not there, himself."

"And you got the blame," Clint said.

"Yes."

"So you moved on."

"Hoping his detectives would not find us again."

"And do you think they have?"

"We did not kill that rancher," Milosh said, "but we will be blamed for it."

"So you believe Ayesha's father's men are in town?"

"Yes."

And he had left her there alone. He only hoped she'd stayed in his room.

"Is that where she is?" Varna asked, as if reading his mind.

"Yes," he said. "I better get back."

He stood and hurried to Eclipse. Varna followed.

"Clint," Varna said, putting her hand on his leg, "bring her back."

"So you can sell her back to her father?"

"Is that what she thinks?" Varna asked.

"Yes," Clint said, "that's what she thinks."

Chapter Thirty-One

The entire situation had changed for Clint. He wasn't really concerned with who killed the rancher, Osborne. That was Marshal Fredericks' problem. He was now concerned solely with Ayesha's safety, whether she was threatened by Osborne's men, or her wealthy birth father.

Before leaving the gypsy camp, he had two more things to talk to Milosh about.

The first was some advice: "Move your camp again. The foreman of the Osborne ranch knows you're here."

The second was a question: "What is Ayesha's father's name?"

"We didn't know his name until his men came to Silverton," Milosh admitted. "He is Vincent Moreland. I do not know his business, but he is very rich."

Clint could find out about the man with one telegram.

He rode back to Rock Springs and immediately checked on Ayesha in his room. Thankfully, she was still there.

"You're back!" she said, looking relieved. "Did you find them?"

"I did," he said. "We talked."

"About my father?"

"Yes."

"They admitted stealing me?"

"Rescuing you, as you said," Clint corrected.

"What did Varna say?"

"I spoke to Varna and to King Milosh," Clint said. "They both seem to love you, Ayesha."

She hugged herself, as if cold.

"Then why do they want to sell me back?"

"They say you misunderstood what you heard," Clint answered.

"I thought it was very clear," she said, "Milosh told Varna the only way to escape from my rich father was to give me back—but to make him pay!"

"Giving you back *would* be a way to satisfy the man, but that doesn't mean they're going to do it."

"Then what will they do?" she asked.

"Talk to him, I guess," Clint said. "Try to reason with him, although . . ."

"Although what?"

"If he really did burn down a town to make a point, he doesn't seem the kind of man you can reason with. But my question would be . . . why does he want you back so badly after all this time?"

"I don't know."

***

In another part of town, two men were eating a late breakfast in the dining room of the best hotel in town, the Spring House.

"Do you think this is going to work?" Greg Garrison asked his companion.

"If not," Tim Simmons said, "we'll just have to try something else, won't we?"

"Nothing as drastic as Silverton, I hope," Garrison said.

"Well, that's not going to be up to us, is it?" Simmons responded.

"When will you find out?"

"After breakfast I'll send a telegram to New York," Simmons said. "We should know by this afternoon."

"Arson and murder," Garrison said. "Why does Mr. Moreland want this girl so badly?"

Simmons cut into his steak-and-eggs and said, "That isn't for us to know, is it?"

Chapter Thirty-Two

"What should we do?" Ayesha asked him.

"We better talk to the marshal."

"Why?"

"Well, for one thing he might know if there are any strangers in town," Clint said. "Strangers who work for your father."

"Did you find out my father's name?"

"Yes," Clint said, "it's Vincent Moreland."

"Who is he?"

"That's something else we're going to find out," Clint said. "I need to send a telegram."

"And what should I do?" she asked.

"You," he said, "are going to stay with me every step of the way."

"Good!"

"Come on," he said, "we'll send the telegram first, then go and see the marshal."

He took her hand and led her from the room.

***

They found the telegraph office and went inside. Normally he would have sent a telegram to his friend

Rick Hartman in Labyrinth, Texas for some information, but Rick had left that town and hadn't settled anywhere else, yet.

He could've sent one to Talbot Roper in Denver but didn't know how that would get him information about a man who lived in New York. He finally decided to just send a telegram to New York to a private detective he knew named Delvecchio. The man lived in Brooklyn, but he'd be able to come up with the information.

Ayesha sat and waited on a wooden bench while he wrote the telegram and waited for the clerk to send it. The clerk kept stealing glances at the girl. Clint hoped it was because she was pretty, not because he thought she was a gypsy. She didn't have the dark hair and skin of a gypsy, but she was wearing the right clothes. Clint wondered if he should stop at the mercantile with her and buy her a new dress.

"It's sent," the clerk told him.

"Thanks. Could you bring any reply to my hotel, please?"

"Sure thing, Mr. Adams."

He turned to Ayesha and said, "Let's go."

Once outside, they headed for the marshal's office. When they got there, she balked.

"It's all right," he said.

"He won't arrest me?"

"No," Clint said, "he won't arrest you."

He put his arm around her and guided her inside.

Marshal Fredericks was seated at his desk and looked up as they entered.

"Is this her?" he asked. "The gypsy girl?"

"It's her," Clint said, "but she's not a gypsy."

"She's the one they chased, right?"

"Right."

"How can you say she's not a gypsy?"

"That's going to take a bit of explaining," Clint said. "Can we sit?"

"Pull those two chairs over," Fredericks said, "and start talkin'."

They sat and Clint explained everything he had learned from Ayesha, and from Milosh and Varna.

"So this rich man from New York burned down Silverton because he wants his daughter back after eighteen years?"

"I know it sounds crazy," Clint said.

"And you think he's in town?" Fredericks asked.

"A man like that sends others to do his dirty work," Clint said. "Do you know if there are any strangers in town?"

"There are a few," the marshal said.

"Have you talked to them?"

"I've been a little busy."

"Maybe you can tell me where they're staying," Clint said, "and I'll talk to them."

"Does she know—"

"Talk to her," Clint said. "If you have questions, talk to her. Her name's Ayesha."

"Ayesha, do you know what this man—your father—looks like?" Fredericks asked.

"No."

"But he's your father."

"I—I don't remember."

"She was about two when the gypsies took—rescued her," Clint said. "Do you remember when you were two years old?"

"No," Fredericks said. "Clint, did you warn the gypsies about the Osborne men?"

"I did."

"Are they gonna move their camp?"

"I hope so," Clint said. "I told them to."

"How will we find them, again?"

"Same way we did before," Clint said. "Don't worry about that. We need to find out if there are any Moreland people in town, Marshal."

"Do you think they killed Osborne?"

"I don't know why they would," Clint said. "How would they even be connected?"

"Well," Fredericks said, "I have to keep lookin' for whoever killed him, not for this girl's father."

"That's fine," Clint said, "just tell me how many strangers there are in town, and where to find them. I'll do the rest."

Chapter Thirty-Three

Ayesha and Clint left the marshal's office.

"He wasn't very helpful, was he?" she asked.

"He's got his job to do," Clint said. "At least he told us something."

"About the strangers?"

"Yes."

"But he's not going to help us talk to them."

"They'll talk to us," Clint said. "Believe me."

They started walking away from the office.

"Ayesha, I'm going to give you a choice," he said. "You can go back to the hotel, or you can come with me. But you have to know one or more of these strangers might end up being the ones who work for your dad."

"But they won't know what I look like, will they?"

"Probably not, but just the fact that you're a young girl—" he started, but she cut him off.

"I will stay with you," she said. "You will keep me safe."

"Yes, I will," he said. "All right, then, let's go and see some strangers."

***

They stopped in front of the Blue Mountain Hotel.

"The marshal said there's one stranger staying here," Clint said.

"But he didn't know his name."

"We'll ask the desk clerk. Come on."

They went into the hotel and crossed the empty lobby to the front desk. The hotel had a beautiful name, but a tacky, dusty lobby.

"Can I help you folks?" an equally dusty, middle-aged clerk asked.

"Yes," Clint said. "My name's Clint Adams, and Marshal Fredericks sent me here."

"Clint . . . Adams?" the clerk said. "The Gunsmith?"

"That's right."

"W-what can I do for you, sir?"

"The marshal told me there was a stranger in town who was staying here."

"That's right," the clerk said. He opened the register. "A Mister . . . Lockwood."

"Is he in his room?"

"I believe so."

"What's the number?"

"He's in room eleven," the clerk said. "Upstairs."

"Thanks."

Clint and Ayesha went up the stairs.

Mr. Lockwood was obviously not working for Ayesha's father, just as he obviously wasn't a killer. He was a
small, sweaty man who sold women's clothing.

***

Their next stop was the Spring House. Fredericks told
them it was the most expensive hotel in town, and that
two well-dressed men had disembarked from the stage a
couple of days ago and checked in.

"Well-dressed and staying in the best hotel in town,"
Clint said to Ayesha. "These may be the men we're
looking for."

This time the clerk was a young man, not nervous or
sweaty, but still impressed by Clint when he found out
who he was.

"Would you like to see the register, sir?" the young
man asked.

"Just tell me the strangers names and room numbers,"
Clint replied.

"Yes, sir."

Once again, they went up the stairs to the second
floor. The two men each had their own room. That suited
Clint. He liked the idea of talking to them separately, if
possible.

First, they went to room seven to see a man named Greg Garrison. When the door opened to Clint's knock, a tall man in his early forties stared at both of them with raised eyebrows.

"Yes? Can I help you folks?"

"My name's Clint Adams. The marshal usually checks on new arrivals, but he's been a little busy and asked me to come and talk to you."

"That right? Are you a deputy?"

"No," Clint said, "I'm just helping out."

"Well," the man said, "I suppose you should come in. Both of you."

As he stepped aside for them to enter, Clint's eyes scanned the room for weapons. Garrison closed the door and turned to face them. The room had a large bed, a couple of overstuffed chairs, a very large chest of drawers and a sidebar, which the man walked to.

"Can I offer you a drink?" he asked. "Is this girl old enough to drink?"

"Never mind," Clint said. "We don't need a drink. We just need to ask you a few questions."

"Very well," Greg Garrison said, "ask your questions."

Chapter Thirty-Four

"What are you doing in town?"

"I represent a man back East," Garrison said. "He's looking for businesses to purchase out here in the West."

"Why?"

"Why? He wants to diversify." He waved his hands. "Spread out his holdings."

"Are you here with anyone else?"

"My partner is in a room across the hall," Garrison said. "His name is Tim Simmons."

"Your partner," Clint said. "What are you—are you—"

"We're lawyers," Garrison said.

"And what's your client's name?"

"I'm afraid I'm not at liberty to divulge that," Garrison said. "Not right now. Once we find a going concern that we can make an offer on, we'll bring up his name as the purchaser. Until then . . ." He shrugged. Clint noticed that Garrison never looked at the girl, which was odd. Men always looked at pretty girls.

"So how long will you be in town?" Clint asked.

"Until we find something."

"Do you have any objections to our talking to your partner?" Clint asked.

"None," Garrison said, "but he's just going to tell you the same thing I did."

"I have to tell the marshal I spoke to both of you."

"Be my guest," Garrison said. "He's right across the hall."

"Do you want to come along?"

"There's no need," Garrison said. "He'll corroborate my story whether I'm there or not."

Clint turned and opened the door but stopped as Ayesha stepped into the hall.

"One more thing," he said.

"Yes?"

"Where are you fellas from?" Clint said.

"Didn't I tell you?"

"You only said you were from back East."

"New York City," Garrison said. "We're from New York."

"Thanks for talking to us," Clint said.

"No problem."

Clint stepped into the hall with Ayesha and closed the door. Then he walked across the way and knocked. This time the door was opened by a shorter, more slender man about the same age as Garrison.

"Are you Mr. Simmons?" Clint asked.

The man looked at Ayesha before answering, "Yes."

"My name is Clint Adams . . ." Clint started, and gave the man the same story they had given his partner about being sent over by the marshal.

"You better come in, then," Simmons said. "I assume you've spoken with my partner. I don't know how much more I can add."

The room was set up in much the same way Garrison's was. And both men kept them very neat. They all sat in chairs.

"Your partner explained that your lawyers looking for business opportunities for your client."

"I couldn't have put it better myself," Simmons said, stealing a look at Ayesha again. Apparently, he was not as successful as his partner in ignoring her presence.

"Is there anything else you might tell me that your partner didn't?" Clint asked. "Like the real reason you're here?" Clint suggested.

"And what would that be, other than what we've told you?" Simmons asked. "I mean . . ." the man leaned forward in his chair, ". . . why do you think we're here?"

"I think," Clint said, "there's something you're not telling anyone—at least, not until you're ready."

"Interesting," Simmons said. "Maybe you should tell the marshal that next time he should come over, himself."

"And you'll have more to tell him?"

"Oh, no," Simmons said, "we'll tell him the same thing, but then he'd be doing his job instead of sending you to do it."

* * *

"Lawyers," Clint said, later.

He and Ayesha left the hotel, stopped in a small cafe down the street. He asked if she wanted tea, but she wanted coffee, so that's what they both had, along with some pie.

"What kind?" she asked Clint.

"Peach," he said. "You'll like it."

The waitress brought them each a slice of peach pie and a cup of coffee. He waited until she took a bite.

"Well?"

"It's wonderful," she said.

"Good," he said. "Eat it slow. We're in no hurry."

"What will we do now?" she asked. "Do you think those men work for . . . for my father?"

"I do," Clint said. "They admitted they're from New York, and they and the little drummer are the only strangers in town, according to the marshal."

"So what will we do now?" she asked, again.

"I think you have to talk to Milosh and Varna," Clint said. "They need to tell you the truth—all of it. Do you think you're ready for that?"

"Yes," she said, nodding, "but after another piece of pie."

Chapter Thirty-Five

When they left the café Ayesha asked, "Are we going out to the camp now?"

"No, it's too late," Clint said. "We wouldn't get back before dark. We'll head out tomorrow morning. That way, if they moved the camp, I can track them in the light."

She fell quiet as they walked back to his hotel.

"Are you all right?" he asked.

"I don't know," she said. "I'm worried."

"About what?"

"About what will happen to Milosh and Varna if they do not send me back to my father," she said, "and what will happen if they do."

"I guess the first thing you should do is find out which of those things you actually need to worry about," Clint said. "Wouldn't that be better than worrying about both of them?"

"Yes."

"All right," he said, "so we'll go talk to Milosh and Varna and find out the truth."

"What about the man who was killed?" she asked. "Do you think those two men did it?"

"I can't see why they would."

"Or someone from the camp?"

"Again, why? Osborne wasn't even one of the men who was chasing you. His death doesn't have anything to do with you."

When they got to the hotel, he told her, "I'd like you to wait in the room for me. I'll come and collect you later for supper."

"What are you going to do?" she asked.

"I've still got some people to talk to, but they won't be people you want to see."

"Those men who chased me?"

"The foreman," Clint said, "but the others might be around. So just relax as much as you can, and I'll be back in a little while."

She looked dubious, but said, "All right."

He stood there in the lobby and watched her go up the stairs, then turned to leave the hotel, but at that moment the clerk caught his eye and waved him over.

"This came for you a little while ago, sir," the clerk said, and handed him a telegram.

"Thank you."

He took the telegram outside with him and opened it. It was from Delvecchio and confirmed what he knew. Vincent Moreland was a rich man from New York who had many businesses, and who lost a girl child in Manhattan when she was only two. He had been looking for her ever since. Vincent Moreland was a man who didn't like losing what was his and swore to get her back no matter what, or when.

He folded the telegram and put it in his pocket. Could a man want his daughter back, not because he loved her, but just because she was his? Like property?

He was trying to decide whether or not to ride out to the Circle K when he heard the horses coming into town. He turned, looked up the street and saw the foreman, Drury, leading a phalanx of riders into town. They were almost riding like a mounted army Calvary patrol. They rode to the marshal's office and reined in. None of them dismounted except for Drury, who went into the office.

Clint crossed the street and approached the riders. As he did, he saw the one called Lonny notice him and alert the others.

"What's going on, boys?" he called out.

They all looked at him, then at Lonny. There had to be a dozen of them.

"You bury your boss this morning?" he asked.

"Yeah, we did," Lonny said. "What of it?"

"Nothing," Clint said. "I was just curious what would bring you to town after doing that?"

"Ain't none of your business is it?" Lonny asked.

"Maybe not," Clint said. "Maybe I'll just go on into the marshal's office and find out if it is."

He stepped up onto the boardwalk and entered the office.

". . . just tellin' you what we're doin', marshal, so you can't say later you didn't know nothin' about it."

As Clint closed the door, both men turned to look at him.

"Clint," Fredericks said.

"This is private, Adams," Drury said.

"Is that why you've got a dozen men sitting outside, waiting for you?" Clint asked. "Because it's private?" He looked at the marshal. "What's going on?"

"Drury's taking his men out to see the gypsies," Fredericks said.

"I said that's private!" Drury snapped.

"Going out there to do what?" Clint asked.

"To find out if they killed my boss," Drury said.

"What makes you think they did it?"

"They're gypsies, ain't they?" Drury asked. "That's like askin' why you think Apaches kill."

"Gypsies are not Apaches," Clint said.

"They ain't so different."

Clint looked at Fredericks.

"Are you going to let him go out there and cause trouble?"

"I was just about to tell him I was goin' with him," the marshal said.

"Good," Clint said, "so am I."

Chapter Thirty-Six

Clint suggested they go to the gypsy camp in the morning.

"No," Drury said, "we're goin' now."

"We won't get back here til after dark," Clint said.

"I don't care," Drury said. "We're goin' whether you come or not." Drury glared at Clint. "You can't stop me, I've got twelve men."

Fredericks looked at Clint, hoping the Gunsmith wouldn't take that as a challenge.

"All right," Clint said. "Give me time to saddle my horse."

"Same for me," Fredericks said. "We'll meet you out front in twenty minutes."

"If it takes you twenty-one," Drury told them, "we'll be gone. Got it?"

"Got it," Fredericks said.

Drury turned and stormed out.

"I've got to stop at my hotel," Clint said, "then I'll meet you out front."

"He means what he says about twenty-one minutes," Fredericks warned.

"I'll be there."

***

"But you said I couldn't go today," Ayesha said. "You said it would be dark when we got back."

"I know what I said," Clint said, "but these men are going out there now and I have to go with them. You just have to wait here."

"All right," she said. "I'll wait."

"And don't go out."

"No," she said, "I won't."

He left the hotel, walked Eclipse over to the marshal's office. The lawman was waiting there with his horse. He was alone.

"Where are they?" Clint asked. "The saloon?"

"They're gone," Fredericks said.

"It's been twenty-one minutes?" Clint asked.

"Twenty-five, Clint."

"We have to catch up to them!"

They both mounted up and lit out.

***

They caught up to the men a couple of miles outside of town.

"Hold up, there!" Fredericks called.

The thirteen riders—Drury and his twelve hands—reined in.

"I told you we wouldn't wait," the foreman said.

"When we get to this camp," Fredericks said, "I want all your men to keep their guns holstered. You understand?"

"That's gonna be up to those gypsies," Drury said. "If they try anything—"

"Drury, I'll kill the first man who draws a gun," Clint said. "That includes you."

"You gonna let him get away with that threat?" Drury demanded of Fredericks.

"Drury," the lawman said, "I'll kill the *second* man who draws a gun. Just keep that in mind."

"Can we continue on, now?" Drury asked.

They all started forward.

Clint fell into place alongside Drury, and at the head of the column.

"I've got a question for you."

"Go ahead," Drury said.

"Did your boss do business with a man named Moreland? From back East?"

"Moreland?" Drury asked. "That name don't sound familiar. Why?"

"He's got two men in town, claim they're lawyers looking for investments for their boss," Clint said. "I'm wondering if they talked with your boss."

"Lawyers," Drury said. "The boss hated lawyers, did all his own legal work. I don't even think he'd talk to 'em."

"Well," Clint said, "I had a feeling they might be more than lawyers."

"Like what?"

"A couple of strongarm types who think they can come here and flex their muscles."

"That wouldn't've worked on the boss, either," Drury said. Abruptly, he turned his head and looked at Clint. "You thinkin' they killed him?"

"I can't say for sure," Clint said, "but it makes more sense to me than gypsies."

"The boss would never sell out to an Easterner," Drury said. "He hated 'em. So . . . maybe you're right."

"You let the marshal know if anyone comes to you looking to buy," Clint said. "Did your boss have relatives to leave the place to?"

"There's a son somewhere, I think," Drury said. "He had a will in his desk, but I ain't looked at it, yet."

"Maybe you better," Clint said. "What are the chances he left the place to you?"

"I dunno," Drury said, "but I can tell ya, if he did, I ain't sellin'—especially not to an Easterner!"

Chapter Thirty-Seven

When they reached the campsite, they saw that all of the wagons had moved.

"You warned 'em!" Drury accused Clint.

"How could I?" Clint asked. "I just found out you were coming out here. Why would I ride with you if I knew they weren't here?"

One of Drury hands came riding up to him.

"The wagons split up when they left here, boss," he said.

"Well," Drury said, "we *could* track 'em, but . . ."

"But what?" Clint asked.

"I'm thinkin' about them two lawyers from back East," Drury said. "Maybe I should talk to 'em."

"Maybe you should," Fredericks said.

"You want us to track 'em, boss?" Lonny said. "Saylor can do that."

"No," Drury said, "we're headin' back."

Clint and Fredericks exchanged a relieved glance. Both were pleased with the way this had gone, so far.

"Head back to town!" Drury called out, then looked at Clint and Fredericks. "You comin'?"

***

It was getting dark when they all rode into Rock Springs. Since the gypsy camp had been moved and they had ridden directly back, they made it before complete darkness fell.

"You boys can go over to the Pretty Lady," Drury said, "or get somethin' to eat."

"Can we go back to the ranch?" one of them asked.

"Not yet," Drury said. "I'll tell you when." He looked at Lonny. "Pick out three men and wait here."

"Sure, boss."

Clint and Fredericks had stopped in front of the marshal's office and gone inside. Drury walked over there and entered. Clint and Fredericks were each sitting with a cup of coffee in their hand.

"What now?" Fredericks asked.

"Those two lawyers Adams told me about," Drury said. "I need their names, and where they're stayin'."

Fredericks looked at Clint.

"Why not?" Clint asked. "In fact, I'll take him over there." He stood up.

"Fine with me," Fredericks said. "I'm gonna finish my coffee."

"Come on," Clint said to Drury, who followed him outside.

"What's wrong with him?" the foreman asked.

"It's his job to find out who killed your boss," Clint said, "and he's got no idea how to do it."

"Do you?"

"Ask questions," Clint said. "That's the only way."

"You really don't think the gypsies did it?"

"No."

"Why not?"

"I spent some time with them," Clint said.

"But gypsies . . . all the stories," Drury said.

"They're just stories."

"So you believe they're innocent."

"Of the murder, yes," Clint said. "I don't know why, I just do."

"Wait."

They were crossing the street when Drury put his hand on Clint's arm to stop him. They had to duck out of the way of a passing buckboard, and the driver cursed them out.

"What about Silverton?" Drury asked. "The story about gypsies burnin' down the town?"

"I don't believe that, either."

"But so many people—"

"So many people tell stories about me that aren't true," Clint said, cutting him off. "Come on, let's get out of the street."

They finished crossing to the other side.

"Where are these lawyers stayin'?" Drury asked.

"Best place in town."

"The Spring House?" Drury said. "That takes a lot of money. They have running water in those rooms."

"Had your boss ever stayed there?"

"No, but when people came to town to see him, if they didn't stay on the ranch, he put them there."

They started walking.

"You've talked to these two?" Drury asked.

"I did," Clint said.

"What did you find out?"

"Not much, just that they're looking for opportunities for their boss. Or so they say."

"Did you believe them?"

"Not entirely."

"So you're not as sure about them as you are about the gypsies."

"No, I'm not."

When they got to the Spring House, they stopped in front.

"Do you wanna come up with me?" Drury asked.

"No," Clint said, "I'll let you talk to them yourself, come to your own conclusions."

"Meet me at the Pretty Lady in an hour, then," Drury said. "We'll talk."

"I'll be there."

Chapter Thirty-Eight

Clint went to the hotel to tell Ayesha what was happening.

"Are you going to look for them?" she asked.

"You and I are, yes," Clint said. "Tomorrow, as planned."

"Can we go eat now?"

"Yes, we'll eat downstairs, but it'll have to be quick. I'm going to meet a man in a little under an hour."

"What man?"

"I'll tell you," he said, opening the door, "over supper."

***

"So you are going to help this man, this foreman?" Ayesha asked, after Clint finished his story.

"Well, I don't believe your people—the gypsies— killed Kenneth Osborne, but the only way I can prove that is to find out who did."

"You think my father is involved?" she asked. "And his two men? The lawyers?"

"If they are lawyers, but yes," Clint said, "I do. It's too much of a coincidence that they're here when Osborne's killed. I hate coincidences."

"But I still need to know the truth," she said, "about everything."

"Were you and your people around Silverton when it burned?" Clint asked her.

She looked down at the steak on her plate and said, "Yes, and everyone thought that Milosh and the others did it."

"So you all had to run."

"Yes."

"You know," Clint said, "there's something that puzzles me."

"And what is that?"

"Why am I so sure the gypsies aren't guilty?" he asked. "I mean, they do lie, cheat and steal, don't they?"

She put her utensils down, sat back and looked at him, squaring her shoulders.

"Yes, they do."

"Then why do I think they didn't kill Osborne? Or burn Silverton?"

"I told you about Varna and her love spells," Ayesha said. "She sleeps with a man, and he is hers. You did sleep with her, didn't you?"

"I did," he said, "but I don't feel I'm under any spell."

"Maybe just not her spell."

"You mean . . . the old woman?" Clint asked.

"Ethelinda," Ayesha said, with a nod.

"You think Ethelinda cast a spell over me?"

"It's like you ask," she said, "why are you so sure Milosh is innocent?"

"So you mean, he's not?" Clint asked. "And I just feel he is because of a spell?"

"Yes," she said. "For if you are under a spell, then that means that Milosh might have done those things."

"But you don't think he did."

"No."

"Would they cast a spell over you?" Clint asked.

"They do not do it to their own people."

"But as you say, you're not a gypsy."

"They feel I am one of their own," she said.

"So tell me," Clint said, "how do I know whether or not I'm under a spell?"

"You cannot tell," she said, "but you have one thing in your favor."

"And what's that?"

"You don't believe in gypsy spells," she said, "do you?"

"No," he said, "I don't. Now finish your supper. I have to get going."

She picked up her knife and fork.

***

When Clint entered the Pretty Lady, he saw some of the Circle K men at a table, but he didn't see Drury, or Lonny.

He approached the table, saw that there were eight men seated at two tables pushed together.

"The rest of you go back to the ranch?" he asked.

"No," one of them said, "they're around . . . some-where."

"And Drury?"

"The boss had somethin' to do," another man said.

"I know," Clint said, "he asked me to meet him here when he was done."

"Then I guess you better wait around," another man said.

"At the bar," someone else said. "Wait at the bar."

"Yeah, right," Clint said, and went to the bar. "Beer."

"Sure," the bartender said.

Clint was halfway through his beer when the batwing doors swung open, and five men walked in, with Drury in the lead. They were all laughing and slapping each other on the back. Clint thought he saw blood on their clothes.

"What the hell did you do?" he asked Drury.

Chapter Thirty-Nine

"Drinks for all my men!" Drury shouted, ignoring Clint as he got to the bar.

"Drury," Clint said, "I asked you a question."

The foreman turned to Clint, who saw that the man had a bruise high on one cheek.

"I decided to take a few of my men with me to talk to those two lawyers, Adams," the foreman said, reaching for his beer. "They didn't really wanna talk to us, so we hadda persuade them."

Clint looked at the other men who appeared disheveled despite their good humor.

"Did you kill either of them?" Clint asked.

"Naw," Drury said, "we just roughed 'em up some, to try to find out what they were doin' here."

"And?"

"Looks like it's the way you said," Drury admitted. "They're looking for opportunities to buy into for their boss. But they're a little more than just lawyers—at least, the big one is. He sorta held his own for a while, but eventually we beat 'im down."

"Well, seems to me if they're on the level and had nothing to do with your boss's murder, they'll be reporting you and your men to the marshal."

"I guess we'll just have to see about that, won't we?" Drury said.

He walked away from Clint with his beer in hand and joined his men in their celebration.

If the gypsies didn't kill Osborne, and the men from the East didn't, then who did? That was still the question.

***

Clint kept watching the batwing doors, waiting for Marshal Fredericks to come in looking for Drury and his men, but it didn't happen. Eventually, the foreman and his men left to return to their ranch. Clint didn't know if Drury still had plans to go out and find the gypsies.

Clint ordered himself another beer and thought about the conversation he had with Ayesha about gypsy spells. Although he had experienced many odd things in his life—including some Indian mysticism—she was right that he didn't believe in spells. What, then, explained his feeling that the gypsies were innocent? He had no facts about Silverton, and since the town had burned down, he had no way of checking to see if the two Eastern lawyers had ever been there.

He decided to pack it in, go back to his room and get some sleep. He and Ayesha could start out early in the morning. Maybe the answers were with the gypsies, after all.

***

Clint and Ayesha had breakfast the next morning, then walked to the livery where Clint rented her a horse, a gentle mare. He saddled both the mare and Eclipse, and they rode out of town. He decided not to check in with the marshal.

"Where are we going?" Ayesha asked, as they rode out of town.

"Back to the last place they camped."

"But they're not there anymore."

"We'll track them from there," Clint said. "We'll find them."

"And then what?"

"And then we get them to talk," Clint said, "about you, about Silverton, about Rock Springs . . . about everything."

"Tell the truth," she said.

"Yes."

"Clint, I might not be a gypsy," she said, "but I've lived with them long enough to know."

"Know what?"

"That telling the truth doesn't come easy to them," she said. "It's almost . . . painful."

"Well, we're just going to have to convince them to start."

***

Marshal Fredericks rode to the Circle K ranch and dismounted. There was nobody in the corral, nobody in the barn, so he walked to the house and knocked on the door. When there was no answer, he walked to the bunkhouse and threw the door open. Inside he heard the sound of snoring, saw that most of the bunks were occupied.

"Drury!" he shouted. "Is Drury here?"

The snoring stopped and men started lifting their heads to see what all the noise was. Fredericks looked at the man nearest him and said, "Jim Drury."

The man in the bunk squinted and pointed. Fredericks walked to the next bunk and looked down at the foreman.

"Wake up, Drury!" he yelled.

The foreman opened his eyes.

"What the—"

"Get up," Fredericks said. "You're under arrest."

Chapter Forty

When Clint and Ayesha reached the campsite, he chose one set of wagon tracks and started to follow them. Looking around, he was sure no one from the Circle K was in the area, and that nobody had followed them.

"See the tracks?" he asked.

"I see them," Ayesha said. "Are you a good . . . what do you call it . . . tracker?"

"No, not particularly," Clint said, "but these tracks are pretty easy to follow."

She fell silent. He had the feeling she didn't want to find where the gypsies had gone.

***

Early in the afternoon they topped a rise and found themselves looking down at the camp.

"All right," he said, "now we're getting somewhere."

"Clint?"

"Yes?"

Ayesha looked at him.

"Will you talk to Milosh?"

"Yes, I will," Clint said, "but you'll have to talk to him at some point, Ayesha. And to Varna. I mean, you've told me they think of themselves as your mother and father."

"Yes," she said, "they have been good to me, but . . . I don't want to be a gypsy."

"That's really something you're going to have to take up with them."

"I'm nineteen," she said. "I don't need their permission to leave."

"But it would be nice to have their support."

She fell silent again, and they rode down into the center of camp. Some of the children came running over, happy to see Ayesha back. The adults just watched them ride in. They didn't rein their horses in until they reached Milosh's wagon.

"Ayesha!"

The girl turned, saw Varna hurrying over. She dismounted and the older woman grabbed her in a tight hug.

"We've been so worried," Varna said.

"I'm sorry," she said. "I had to get away . . . to think."

Varna looked up at Clint.

"Thank you for bringing her back."

"I didn't so much bring her back as we rode out here together, to see you and Milosh," Clint said.

"Step down, then," Varna said. "I will get Milosh."

Clint dismounted and stood next to Ayesha as Varna walked off. The young man named Vano, who had cared for Eclipse before, came over to take their horses.

"Where's Ethelinda's wagon?" Clint asked Ayesha.

"That one, there, on the end," she said. "Away from all the others. You're going to talk to her?"

"I think so," Clint said. "I want to see about this spell business."

"Just don't call her a fraud," Ayesha advised him. "She would take that as a challenge and bring disaster down upon you to prove her point."

"Thanks for the warning."

Varna reappeared with Milosh following behind her.

"Ayesha," he said, and hugged her. "We were worried."

"I am sorry."

Milosh looked at Clint.

"You wanted to talk to me?"

"I want us all to talk," Clint said. "You, me, Varna, Ayesha . . . and maybe Ethelinda."

Milosh looked grim.

"If you want to talk to Ethelinda, you will have to do it alone, in her wagon," the King said.

"That's fine," Clint said, "but we can talk first."

Milosh and Varna exchanged a glance.

"Very well," Milosh said, "come to my wagon."

The King led the way, followed by Clint, Ayesha and Varna.

When they reached his wagon, Clint saw that the man had a fire going.

"Sit," Milosh said, "and tell me what is on your mind."

"The truth is on my mind, Milosh," Clint said. "Is that something you can handle?"

"But of course," Milosh said. "There are people who believe that the truth is foreign to gypsies. Some of those people are even gypsies themselves. But do you know what gypsies are, Clint?"

"I've heard many things," Clint said.

"We are travelers," Milosh said. "That is all. You, yourself, spend much time on the trail, no?"

"I do," Clint confirmed.

"Some might call you a gypsy."

"It hasn't happened yet," Clint said, "but I suppose you're right."

"So what gypsy myth do you wish me to dispel by telling the truth?" the King asked.

"I'd like you to tell Ayesha the truth about her father, and where she comes from."

"Is this what you wish, Ayesha?" Milosh asked.

"Yes," Ayesha said, lifting her chin, "it is."

"Very well, then," Milosh said.

Chapter Forty-One

"We have always told you that we rescued you," Milosh said to Ayesha, "and we did, but . . . as far as the *Gadjo* law is concerned, we stole you."

"Why?" she asked.

Varna answered. "Your father was a brutal man who beat your mother, in private and in public. We were there, on the street, when he hit you, and that's when we took you."

"We left New York the next day to come west," Milosh said. "He has been looking for you ever since."

"Why?" Clint asked. "Why all these years?"

Milosh looked at Clint.

"Because someone took something that was his," Milosh said. "He will not stop until he has it—Ayesha—back."

"You would sell me back to him for profit?" she asked.

"Clint said you thought you heard something like that," Milosh said. "No, we would never do that. You are our *Chaivis*." He looked at Clint and translated. "She is our child."

"I see."

Varna, sat next to Ayesha, put her arms around the girl and hugged her.

"Milosh, how many times has Vincent Moreland caught up to you?"

"He seems to find us every few years," Milosh said. "He uses the Pinkertons."

Clint nodded. The two men calling themselves "lawyers" certainly fit the bill as "Pinkertons."

"Milosh," Clint said, "I need to speak to Ethelinda."

Milosh and Varna exchanged a quick look.

"Ethelinda?" he said. "She does not speak with *Gad-jo.*"

"Really?" Clint asked. "I thought you folks told fortunes all the time."

"Another myth," the King of the gypsies said.

"Is it a myth that she cast a spell on me to make it easy for me to decide to help you, and believe in you?"

"What?" Milosh asked.

"Let him talk to her," Varna said. Milosh looked at her. "It is the only way he will see how silly he is being."

"Very well," Milosh said, getting to his feet. "Come with me."

He led Clint to the wagon Ayesha had pointed to.

"Wait here."

Milosh climbed into the wagon, then reappeared moments later and dropped down to the ground.

"You can go in," Milosh said. "She is ready for you."

"Thanks."

"Just remember," Milosh said, "she is an old woman from the old country."

"I'll remember."

Clint turned to the wagon.

"Hello? I'm coming in."

He climbed into the back of the wagon. The inside was dark, lit by a single lamp with a low flame. Then, abruptly, the flame got higher, lighting the interior. When Milosh said she was an old woman, he wasn't kidding. She had long gray hair, a heavily lined face that had amazingly clear blue eyes shining out from it. She looked as if she was clad in various multi-colored veils.

"Ethelinda?"

She was sitting at a small table.

"Sit."

There was a chair across from her, which he sat in. The interior of this wagon was larger than most that he had been inside.

"The King says you have questions," she said, pronouncing it "gvestions."

"That's right."

There was a deck of cards on the table in front of her, unlike any he had seen before. They were larger than most, and rather than numbers, they had figures on them.

Not like an American deck, which had Kings, Queens and Jacks. This deck was colorful, and had both human figures, and other things, like buildings and swords.

"What kind of cards are those?"

"These ees the Tarot," she said, picking the cards up. "They tell your future, and your past. Do you want to know your future?"

"No, thanks," Clint said. "I know my future."

"Yes," she said, putting the cards down and staring at him, "I can see that."

"You can?"

"Yes." she nodded. "Your future is . . . a bullet!"

"That's right."

"You cannot escape it."

"I don't expect to," he said.

"That is good," she said. "Eet ees good to know the truth."

"That's why I'm here," Clint said. "To find out the truth."

"Then ask your questions," she said, "and I will do my best to answer them."

"First," Clint said, "did you cast some kind of spell on me?"

Chapter Forty-Two

"I did," Ethelinda said.

He was surprised. It was obviously the truth.

"How did you do it?"

"With a lock of hair Varna gave to me."

"Varna?" She could only have gotten a lock of his hair one way, while they were having sex. He certainly hadn't felt it, but he was busy feeling other things, at the time.

"And what was this spell supposed to do?" he asked.

She leaned forward and said, "Invoke trust."

"It was a . . . trust spell?"

"You might call it that," Ethelinda said. "Milosh and Varna wanted you to trust them and help them."

"I *am* helping," Clint said.

"And are you trusting?" she asked.

"Well, yeah," he said, "but I put that down to my own instincts."

"You may believe what you like."

"How does it work?" he asked. "What did you do with my hair?"

"I burned it," she said.

"So if you removed this spell, I would then suspect the gypsies—stop trusting Milosh and Varna?"

"Yes," she said, "unless you are truly able to depend on your own instincts."

"I usually am," he said.

She frowned at him.

"If your own feelings are strong enough," she said, "the spell would not work."

"Like Varna's spell?"

"Varna?"

"Yes, she was supposed to have put some sort of love spell on me."

"And it did not work," Ethelinda said. It was a comment, not a question, but he answered it, anyway.

"That's right, it didn't."

After a few moments of thought, Ethelinda said, "Then perhaps mine did not work, either."

"How would you know that?"

She abruptly leaned forward and put both her hands on the table, palms up.

"Give me your hands."

He hesitated. If she clamped down on his hands and somebody came rushing in with a gun, he was dead. But this was about trust, wasn't it?

He gave her his hands. She held him by the wrists and examined his palms, then looked up and stared into his eyes.

"You have it," she said.

"Have what?" he asked.

"The instinct," she said, releasing his hands. "It is as you said. Varna's spell and my spell did not work. You have the instinct, and you must trust yourself."

"That's what I've always done, Ethelinda." He stood up. "Thank you."

"Do not thank me," she said. "It is rare I find a *Gadjo* with the instinct. It is I who should thank you."

He turned and left the wagon.

***

Milosh and Varna watched Ayesha as she crouched down by the fire.

"What will we do?" Varna asked. "If she wants to leave?"

"She is old enough to make her own decisions," he said.

"But if she does that, he will find her and take her back," Varna said.

"That will also be up to her."

"No," Varna said, "I will not let her go."

"We could sell her back to him," Milosh said. "She would go home, and we would get rich."

"You do not mean that," Varna said. "We have talked about this before, and you do not mean it."

"No," he said, "I do not."

They turned as Clint approached them.

"What did the old woman say?" Milosh asked.

"Her spell didn't work."

"Then you believe us," Milosh said, "because you feel in your bones you know the truth?"

"Yes."

"Do you also know who killed the rancher?" Milosh asked.

"That's not my problem."

"And Silverton?" Varna asked. "Who burned it?"

"It's as you said," Clint replied, "Ayesha's father would do anything to get her back. And to sully the name of the gypsies."

"Then it was his men?" Milosh asked.

"I'll have to go back to town and question them again," Clint said.

"But why would that be your business if a *Gadjo* murder is not?" Milosh asked.

"If Ayesha decides to stay with you," Clint said, "I want her to have something to stay for."

Chapter Forty-Three

Clint agreed to stay in camp longer, giving Ayesha time to continue to talk with Milosh and Varna before she decided to stay, or return to town with him.

Somebody was kind enough to put on a pot of coffee for Clint, who sat off to one side and drank it while thinking more about his meeting with Ethelinda. She was convinced that spells did exist, they just didn't work on him. He was convinced that spells didn't exist. It didn't matter which of them was right, because the outcome was the same. He was going to depend on his own instincts to make his final decisions.

He watched the adults in camp with their children, and they all seemed very content with their lot in life. They also appeared to be a gentle bunch. Of course, it was possible they were all putting on an act, but he didn't think that was the case.

He went to the fire where the coffee pot was to refill his cup. As he did, he saw a young man come running into camp, and recognized him as the one called Ferka. The young man ran right to Milosh and spoke urgently. Clint walked over to find out what was going on.

"Ferka says there are riders approaching," Milosh said. "More than a dozen."

"Damn," Clint said. "The Circle K bunch are insisting on being stupid."

Drury and his men apparently weren't satisfied with beating the two Pinkertons—if, indeed, the two "lawyers" were Pinkertons. Now they were intent on engaging the gypsies.

"What do we do?" Varna asked. "We have no time to run."

"Do you have any guns in camp?" Clint asked Milosh.

"A few, but they are for hunting small game," he said.

"Okay, forget it, then. I'll have to handle this myself."

"A dozen men?" Ayesha asked.

"Get the children into the wagons," Clint said. "Also the women, and the old folks."

Milosh told Varna, Ayesha and Ferka, "Go! Do as he says!"

"What about you?" Clint asked.

"I am King," Milosh said. "I will get my gun and stand with you."

Clint was about to tell him no when something occurred to him.

"A show of force wouldn't be bad," Clint said. "If you have other men who can shoot, I have extra guns."

"None of us have ever shot anything but game," Milosh pointed out.

"That's all right," Clint said. "They won't know that."

Milosh nodded, went to get his gun, and his men.

***

By the time he heard the sound of the thundering hooves approaching, Clint and Milosh had armed four other men with guns the gypsies had in camp, plus Clint's rifle and Colt New Line.

"Nobody shoots unless I do," Clint instructed them. "And try not to look so scared."

The four men standing behind Clint and Milosh all swallowed and tried to change the expressions on their faces.

"And if there is shooting," Clint said, "you can run if you need to. There'll be no shame."

The young man holding Clint's rifle was Vano, the one who cared so well for Eclipse. He seemed to be the most determined of the men Milosh had chosen to stand with them.

"Six against twelve looks like better odds," Clint commented.

The sound of the horses got closer, and then the riders appeared, led by Jim Drury. He held his hand up to stop his men as he saw Clint standing there.

"You don't wanna be here, Adams," he said.

"What are you doing, Drury?" Clint asked. "I thought I convinced you the gypsies were innocent."

"Gypsies ain't innocent, Adams," Drury said. "Even if they didn't kill our boss, we don't want 'em around here."

"What happened with those two Pinkertons?" Clint said. "I half expected you to be in a jail cell today."

"Fredericks tried that," Drury said. "He came to the ranch this mornin', woke us all up and tried to arrest me."

"Alone?" Clint asked. "Did you kill him?"

"He ain't dead, but he won't be walkin' around for a while."

"You and your men are intent on doling out your own brand of justice, aren't you?"

Drury grinned.

"Those Easterners got it, then the marshal, and I guess you and your gypsy friends are next."

"Only we're not just going to stand here and take it, Drury," Clint said. "You're going to have a fight on your hands."

"So you're gonna stand with them?" Drury waved his hand. "They don't look like much."

"I am," Clint said, "and I'm dead sure I can shoot you out of your saddle first thing, so you won't be around to see how this plays out."

Drury was mulling things over, but his man Lonny was a lot more impatient.

"Oh hell," Lonny said, and drew his gun.

Chapter Forty-Four

Clint had promised to take Drury out of his saddle, but it was Lonny who went flying as Clint's bullet struck him in the chest. Very quickly, he then pointed his gun at Drury, who put his hands up in front of his face.

"Wait! Wait!" the foreman shouted.

"It's your call," Clint said.

All the men behind Drury looked confused and kept their hands away from their guns. Clint heard the men behind him stir, but nobody fired a shot.

"What was your play here, Drury?" Clint asked.

"A show of force," Drury said. "I thought if these gypsies were guilty, they might admit it in the face of all these guns. I didn't expect you to be here."

"And what about your man Lonny being stupid?" Clint asked. "Did you expect that?"

"Let's just say I'm not surprised by it," Drury said, staring down at Lonny.

"What do you want to do now?" Clint asked.

"Talk," Drury said, "just talk. I know when we get back to town I'll probably be arrested. That is, if Fredericks is up and around. But before I get put into a cell, I'd like to have everything figured."

"You expect to know who killed your boss?"

"I at least wanna be sure about the gypsies," Drury said.

"I tell you what," Clint said. "Send your men home and dismount. I think the gypsies are willing to talk to you."

Clint looked at Milosh, who nodded.

Drury turned in his saddle to speak to his men.

"Pick him up and take him back to the ranch with you," he said, pointing to Lonny.

"You sure, boss?" one of the men asked.

"I'm sure."

"What if the marshal comes around again?"

"You tell him if he leaves all the hands alone, I'll turn myself in when I get back to town." Drury looked at Clint. "Tell him I'm with the Gunsmith."

"Right, boss."

All the hands turned their horses and rode away, relief clear in their demeanors.

Clint holstered his gun and said, "Step on down and I'll get you a cup of coffee."

***

Clint drank coffee with Drury and allowed the man to watch the activity in the gypsy camp, the adults working, the children playing.

"So what exactly happened with the Pinkertons?" Clint asked.

"Oh, that," Drury said. "We went to their rooms to ask them some questions. The big one got nasty, threw a punch, which was a mistake. My men beat him down. That's when I went through his pockets and found his Pinkerton badge."

"So they're definitely Pinkertons."

"Well, he is," Drury said. "The other one came running from across the hall, started yelling, and got beat down. I went through his pockets, but he's just a lawyer."

"And both are working for Vincent Moreland?"

"That's the name that was on a telegram I found in the room," Drury said.

"What did it say?"

"That they should do what was necessary."

"To accomplish what?"

"That I don't know," Drury said, "and they weren't in any condition to talk."

"I may have to go and see them myself," Clint said.

"Do you think they killed the boss? I mean, if these people didn't do it."

"If they did, they wanted everyone to think it was the gypsies."

"What do they have against the gypsies?"

"What does anybody have against them? What did you?"

Drury looked around.

"Well, I didn't think they were like this," the foreman said. "I thought they were . . . you know . . . savages."

"Well, they're not," Clint said.

"So you think the Pinkerton did it?"

"I've worked with the Pinkertons," Clint said. "I don't think William or Robert would have sanctioned this kind of murder. If this Pinkerton killed, he probably did it on his own for whatever Moreland is paying him."

"But why?"

"That young girl," Clint said, pointing at Ayesha, "is apparently Moreland's long-lost daughter."

"So if he killed the boss . . ."

". . . it wasn't personal. They must've thought the murder of an important man in town would accomplish their goal. Somehow, incriminating the gypsies, they'd be able to grab the girl."

"That doesn't make any sense," Drury said.

"No, it doesn't," Clint argued. "But when I get back to town, I'll try and *make* sense of it."

Chapter Forty-Five

Clint mounted Eclipse, preparing to ride back to Rock Springs with Jim Drury.

"Will you be coming back?" Ayesha asked.

"Probably not," he said. "Do you want to come with me?"

"Travel with you?" she asked.

"No, no," Clint said, "just leave the gypsies and come to town. What you do after that is up to you. Do you want to go back to your father?"

"No," she said, "I don't know him."

"But you wanted to leave here," Clint said.

She looked around, then back at him and said, "Not anymore. Not since we talked."

Milosh and Varna came over and put their arms around Ayesha.

"Look," Clint said, "if I can get a message back to Moreland through his men, I'll advise him to leave you people alone."

"After all these years?" Milosh asked. "I think we will always be looking over our shoulders."

"I'll see what I can do," Clint said. "It was nice meeting you people." He looked at Drury. "You ready?"

"Let's go," Drury replied. He didn't say goodbye to the gypsies, but it was an indication of how his attitude had changed that he touched the brim of his hat.

***

When they got back to Rock Springs, Clint decided to go to the Spring House Hotel, rather than the marshal's office. If Fredericks was there, he might arrest Drury on the spot.

They dismounted in front of the hotel, entered and went upstairs to room seven to see Greg Garrison, the Pinkerton.

Clint knocked. When Garrison swung the door open, he had a gun in his hand. Clint drew quickly and pointed his gun at the man's face.

"Drop it."

Garrison firmed his jaw.

"Don't be stupid."

Garrison dropped the gun. Clint shoved him into the room, picked up the gun, and closed the door.

"Now, we're going to talk," Clint said.

"About what?"

"Gypsies, for a start," Clint said. "Then murder."

Garrison's face still bore the marks from his encounter with the Circle K boys and Drury.

"I told him—" Garrison started, pointing at Drury, but Clint cut him off.

"You're not dealing with him now," he said. "You're dealing with me."

"Look," Garrison said, "I reported him to the marshal. I can do the same thing to you."

"Sit down, Garrison," Clint said, gesturing with the gun. "Sit."

Garrison sat on the bed, and Drury took up a position standing in a corner to watch.

"You work for Vincent Moreland," Clint said.

"Who?"

"Don't make me search the room for a letter, or telegram, from New York."

Garrison firmed his jaw, again.

"Fine," he said, "so I work for Moreland. So what?"

"Aren't you supposed to be working for the Pinkertons?"

"I left the Pinks."

"Did you?" Clint asked. "Do they know you left? They don't usually let ex-operatives keep their badges."

"I'll be handing in my resignation when I get back," Garrison said.

"Interesting," Clint said. "What makes you think you'll be getting back?"

"Why wouldn't I be?"

"Try murder."

"What murder are you talking about?" Garrison demanded.

"I don't know, could be some people died in that Silverton fire," Clint said. "You know, when you burned down the town? Or could be you killed Kenneth Osborne with a knife, trying to frame the gypsies."

"Why would I do that?"

"To force them into giving up Moreland's daughter."

"Look, it was just my job to find 'er," Garrison said. "You want to talk to somebody about murder, try across the hall."

"Simmons?" Clint asked. "The lawyer?"

"He isn't a damn lawyer," Garrison said. "He's a killer for hire."

"What?" Drury said.

"Yeah," Garrison said, "He uses any means necessary—fire, knives, guns."

"Moreland employs killers?" Clint asked.

"Just one," Garrison said. "Simmons. Uses him whenever he wants to get his way."

"But why Osborne?" Clint asked.

Garrison shrugged.

"He said the more important the victim, the madder the town would get at the gypsies."

"So, killing my boss was just random . . . conven-ient?" Drury demanded.

"Hey, take that up with him across the hall," Garrison said. "I'm leaving town tomorrow. I've had enough."

"What are you going to tell your boss about his daughter?" Clint asked.

"That she's a goddamned gypsy," Garrison said. "Why would he want to bother?"

"Then give him a message from me."

"What's that?"

"If he continues to stalk the gypsies, and his daughter, he's going to have to deal with me."

"Deal with the Gunsmith?"

"That's right," Clint said. "Make sure he knows that."

"I'll tell him."

"And the same goes for you," Clint added.

"Don't worry," Garrison said. "You aren't going to see me again, ever."

"Make sure that's true," Clint said.

"I will."

"But before you leave," Clint said, "you're going to have to make a statement to the marshal, so he can arrest your partner."

"He's not my partner," Garrison said. "I didn't even want to be here with him. I don't want to make a state-ment."

"You either make it," Clint said, "or get arrested with him. Your choice."

"Goddamnit!" Garrison swore.

Chapter Forty-Six

As it turned out, Fredericks took Garrison's statement, arrested Simmons, then arrested Drury, not for beating up the two men from the East, but for administering a beating to the marshal when he tried to arrest him that morning. He took the full brunt of the blame for that, keeping his men from sharing a cell. Clint had the feeling, though, that he'd get off with a fine.

It was Clint's intention to leave town the next day, just as Garrison was going to do. He decided to go back to his room early, now that the gypsies seemed to be in the clear not only for Osborne's murder, but with Ayesha's father, as well. Of course, he couldn't be sure that Moreland would leave his daughter and the gypsies alone, but he hoped that would be the case.

As he approached the door of his room, his instincts kicked in, and he realized somebody was inside. It helped that he could see the light beneath the door, and knew he hadn't left the lamp lit.

He put his left hand on the doorknob and kept his right hand ready to draw his gun.

When he threw the door open, Varna looked up at him from the bed, wide-eyed and naked.

"You startled me," she said.

He stepped inside and closed the door quickly.

"What are you doing here?" he asked, realizing immediately what a stupid question it was.

She leaned back on her hands so he could see every inch of her bountiful body.

"What do you think?" she asked. "I've come to say goodbye."

"Are you sure you didn't come to try your love spell again?" he asked.

"No," she said, "I think I'm here because you cast a spell on me, Clint Adams."

He approached the bed, cradled the heavy undersides of her breasts in his hands, teased her large nipples with his thumbs. She closed her eyes and allowed her head to drop back.

He released her breasts just long enough to get undressed and hang his gunbelt on the bedpost, then went back to her and ran his hands over her curves. She shivered beneath the touch of his fingers.

"Did you do this with Ayesha while she was here?" Varna asked.

"No," Clint said. "She wanted to, but I told her she was too young. Besides, she wouldn't have been able to measure up to your beauty and experience."

She reached down between his legs to stroke him and said, "You know the right things to say, don't you?"

He got onto the bed with her, laid alongside her, pulled her hot body against his and kissed her, sliding one hand down between her thighs to find her wet.

"I didn't have time to take a bath," she said, sheepishly. "I must smell like a mule."

"You smell just fine," he said, as the scent of her wetness reached his nostrils, "and getting sweeter by the minute."

He began to roam her body with his mouth, pausing at each nipple, working his way down, stopping briefly at her deep navel, and then moving on. When he had his face between her thighs he breathed in her odors, sweet and sour, which combined to form something exotic. As he worked on her with his tongue she gasped, reached down to hold his head there, and began to move her hips. Before long she was gushing and moaning, writhing about on the bed.

When he moved his face away from her crotch, he got on top of her, pressed the head of his cock to her wet pussy and plunged into her.

She gasped as he drove his hard cock completely into her, then brought her legs up to wrap them around his waist. Then she started almost chanting in a language he couldn't understand, and he just hoped she wasn't calling some gypsy curse down on him.

Not that he believed in that, at all.

Coming September 27, 2020

THE GUNSMITH
463
The Gunsmith's Women's Club

For more information
visit: www.SpeakingVolumes.us

On Sale Now!

THE GUNSMITH
461
Standoff in Labyrinth

For more information
visit: www.SpeakingVolumes.us

Coming September 2020!

Lady Gunsmith
9
Roxy Doyle and the Lady Executioner

For more information
visit: www.SpeakingVolumes.us

On Sale Now!

Lady Gunsmith
Books 1 - 8
Roxy Doyle and the Silver Queen

On Sale!

**Award-Winning Author
Robert J. Randisi (J.R. Roberts)**

**For more information
visit:** www.SpeakingVolumes.us

www.ingramcontent.com/pod-product-compliance
Lightning Source LLC
Chambersburg PA
CBHW030452250626
47154CB00003BA/1244